"21"

"21"

The Life and Times of New York's Favorite Club

by
Marilyn
Kaytor

THE VIKING PRESS NEW YORK

First published in 1975 by The Viking Press, Inc.
625 Madison Avenue, New York, N.Y. 10022
Published simultaneously in Canada by
The Macmillan Company of Canada Limited
Library of Congress Cataloging in Publication Data
Kaytor, Marilyn. "21": The Life and Times of New York's Favorite Club.
Includes index. 1. Jack and Charlie's "21," New York. I. Title.
TX945.5.J3K39   647'.95747'1   75-15672   ISBN 0-670-73460-8
Printed in U.S.A.

THIS BOOK WAS DESIGNED BY GEORGE KRIKORIAN

Anderson/*The Herald News*, pages 159, 166. The Bettmann Archive, Inc., pages 32, 58. Byron Company, Inc., page 77. Camera Arts Studio, page 134. Don Charles of *The New York Times*, page 109. Cigar Institute of America, page 160. Maxwell Coplan, page 66. Culver Pictures, Inc., pages 2, 3, 24, 27, 29, 61, 82, 83. Walter Daran, pages 117. Alfred Eisenstaedt, opposite page 1 (repeated pages 12, 20, 36, 50, 62, 74, 88, 106, 120, 128, 136, 152, 162), pages 69, 123, 131 bottom, 141, 142, 147 bottom, 154-55 left, 167, 171, 174, 175. Barrett Gallagher, pages 93, 94-95, 102, 122, 144-45. Harcourt-Harris Inc., page 98, middle picture. Max Henriquez, page 108 right, 176. Allan Kain, pages 130 top, 138, 143, 147 top. Jean-Pierre Laffont, page 157. F. S. Lincoln, page 65. Wallace Litwin, page 105. Bill Mark, pages 126, 127, 173. Ross McKelvie, page 135. Mirror Newspapers Limited, page 169. Morgan Photo Service, page 81 right. Morse-Pix, page 57. New York Times Studio, pages 116, 130 bottom, 156, 164. Standard Flashlight Company, Inc., pages 44, 60 top and bottom, 87, 92, 125. Standard Studios, pages 38, 53, 98 top. *Time Magazine*, page 113. "21" Picture File, pages 16, 20, 22, 23, 28 right, 38, 39, 41, 42, 43, 45, 46-47, 53, 54 (all three pictures), 55, 56, 59, 68, 78-79, 86, 90, 97, 98 bottom, 100, 108 left, 110-11, 114-15, 119, 131 top, 140, 148, 149, 151, 155 right, 161, 165, 168, 172. United Press International Photo, pages 5, 6, 9, 25, 49, 101. Gary Wagner Photography, page 99 left. William R. Whitteker Associates Inc., pages 139, 170. Wide World Photos, pages 10, 11, 14-15, 17, 18, 19, 26, 28 left, 40, 48 left and right, 70-71, 72, 73, 76.

Dedication: For Jack and Charlie and Mac and Bob

Acknowledgments

I would like to express appreciation to all those good people who magnanimously gave of their time and recollections and revealed the facts and fancies for this book. I would especially like to thank Edward Irving, Bill Hardey, Harold Alpert, Julius Hallheimer, Herbert Rubsamen, Soll Roehner, Johnny Seeman, Benedict Quinn, Nathaniel Goldstein, and the pseudonymous Murray.

I would also like to thank George Krikorian, the designer of this book, and Barbara Burn, my editor at The Viking Press.

My very special thanks are extended to H. Peter Kriendler, H. Jerome Berns, and Sheldon Jay Tannen, proprietors of "21," their families, and the "21" personnel, all of whom provided valuable information and cooperation in the preparation of this story of The "21" Club.

M.K.

Contents

Introduction

No matter who you are or where you come from, you've heard *something* about it.

Some people know it as Jack & Charlie's, some as "21," and others as just the Numbers Place. Eddie Condon, the man who tamed jazz for popular consumption, used to ring up his friends and say, "Meet me at the Numerical Place at the rich man's dawn and we will have our psyches half-soled." Which freely translated meant, "See you at The '21' Club at 6:00 p.m. and we'll have a drink."

"21" is also fondly known as "the front porch." And for any youngsters who don't know what that means, it used to be said of the Raffles Hotel in Singapore that if you sit on the front porch long enough you'll meet everybody who is anybody.

People agree on its being the front porch. What they can't agree on is *why*. What has gone into the creation of a place that is a legend unto itself?

Restaurant ratings are subjective judgments based on a great number of imponderables. Absolutely vital to a great restaurant's success are the proprietor and his staff, their housekeeping philosophy, and the ambiance —which takes in everything from the "hello" of the doorman to the quality of the coffee to the porter's mood when he sweeps out the men's room. But apart from these, and the fine victuals and healthy-sized drinks, undoubtedly tradition ranks highest as the reason for "21's" success. Pete Kriendler, one of the owners of the place, put his finger on it: "It has developed a patina. You can't just create a place like this. It has to grow, with a little watering here and there, and a lot of love and friendship between owners and clientele."

Forget its reputation for exclusiveness and for being a celebrity trap with a famed and luminous roster of guests. In "21" we find a restaurant whose real crowning achievement is that it has offered to people sagacious of the good life a home away from home—a comfortable rocking chair and plenty of booze in the drinks.

John Steinbeck summed it up by saying, "If you build a better mouse trap, mice will come from all over to enjoy it." But can all mice get in? Lucius Beebe once called "21" not only the most glamorous restaurant in town but also the hardest place in the world to get into. Myth has it that one must show his bank book at the door, and *New York* magazine has said, "Even Cary Grant can be made to feel he has egg on his tie."

But the management is honestly *not* stuffy, though it has been known on rare occasions to invoke banishment from the premises. Regulars remember the story of a young lad who once incurred the wrath of proprietor Charlie and was banished from the club for a year, which he prudently spent in Europe to ease his disgrace. Exactly one year later he returned and happily heralded his entrance into the bar with a loud shout of "Aren't those three-minute eggs done yet?" He was promptly cast out for another year.

The éclat of "21" can be credited to its own essence rather than to any set of rules, emotions, or circumstances which have been molded together to make the "21" mystique. Lois Long once said that one real secret of this house lies in the fact that "every customer who comes in the door is treated like a person who has not yet had his morning coffee." On the other hand, many people feel that the unique quality of the club stems from the attitude and loyalty of the clientele. Apropos of this feeling, President Harry Truman once expressed profound apologies for not coming into "21" more often, explaining that he had just been kept awfully busy down in Washington.

"21" is a very special place; not a bar, not a restaurant, but a great jolly drinking and dining establishment with an aura of self-assurance and an intimate masculine flavor that sets it apart from other gin mills into almost the private club category, yet it doesn't suffer the parochialism of a private club. It is home to those in need of sensitive shelter. The club is not a place for someone with a passion for anonymity, but, on the other hand, the house is so discreet that a lady of note can dine with her lover upstairs while her husband drinks blissfully ignorant at the bar below.

This civilized charm is purveyed by the men who run and own "21," Pete Kriendler, his cousin Jerry Berns (brothers of Jack Kriendler and Charlie Berns, who built this golden mouse trap assisted by Mac and Bob Kriendler, who were also a part of its heritage), and Kriendler nephew Sheldon Tannen. These gentlemen restaurateurs believe in offering not just an eclectic retreat but also a place where busy people can do business amidst a steady round of kisses and handshakes.

Tex McCrary calls "21" "the catalyst on the hot tin roof of this town," and *Forbes* magazine once speculated that more business is done on the floor of "21" than on The Floor. Regulars who trudge faithfully through its famous iron gate after being away for a while know that coming back to town means reading a mountainous stack of *The New York Times* to catch up on the news and then going to "21" to get the rest of it.

"21" not only provides those little things that count but embraces the conviction that a restaurant exists for the pleasure and comfort of its patrons, and a belief in that hoary aphorism that the customer is always right. Why else would they have allowed Harpo Marx, in reply to an unfamiliar dowager's question of "How are you, Mr. Marx?" to stand up on a chair in the conservative upstairs dining room, remove his jacket, tie, and shirt, thump his bared chest, and say, "I'm fine, see?"

The myth of the exclusivity of "21" has given cause for regulars to poke fun at "their club," and this irreverence is one of the true secrets of the house's popularity with its following. Helen Hayes recalls a prank of her late husband, Charles MacArthur, who stood up in the dining room one night, gave a shrill, two-fingered whistle blast, and shouted to the waiter, "Miss Hayes would like her check, please."

Though the club maintains that it is not the most expensive restaurant in town, John Hay ("Jock") Whitney, a man worth too many millions to count, once quipped, "I can't afford the damn place." But don't underestimate the humor of the owners themselves. They are also pranksters off on a spree. Ken Venturi once sent an entrée back to the kitchen and a couple of days later, after he had won the U.S. Open golf championship, returned to "21" and ordered a profiterole dessert. He received three golf balls covered with chocolate sauce.

The story of this famous house is as much a story of its people as it is of wining and dining and bountiful drinks. To this sweet and mysterious world have come the most colorful denizens of five decades. This institution came into being in the age of "the Great Foolishness," as Beebe dubbed Prohibition, and it was into that time of dry agony that there stepped Jack Kriendler and Charlie Berns to break a foolish law and to bring good booze and good cheer to a disconsolate city. Through fate and their own cunning, these two boys were destined to become the most famous saloonkeepers in New York. They offered the most popular speakeasy of Prohibition times, and it became a landmark restaurant after that, where beautiful and relaxed Café Society reigned through the thirties and until after World War II. It was where the expense-account crowd reached stuffed capacity in the fifties, to give way in the early sixties to the present graffiti-like mixture of connoisseurs, jet setters, and the very very rich and famous.

But few people who step thirstily through its doors today know of the humble way this house that Jack and Charlie built began. This book tells the story of how a tiny clandestine retreat turned into the most fashionable and respected saloon in town.

1
Getting Going

The 1920s opened with the delightfully firm belief that life was just a bowl of cherries and New York just this side of paradise. People were fascinated with *style moderne*, the automobile, radio, the silver screen, and ragtime. They dressed, laughed, ate, and drank with flair, and there was always time for a cold cocktail and a leisurely, long, and luxurious dinner in one of the big "entrance" restaurants that huddled around Broadway in midtown. The list is an impressive one: Sherry's, Shanley's, Reisenweber's, Rector's, and Bustanoby's Café des Beaux Arts—where "Reggie" Vanderbilt brought a hansom cab horse as a guest to dinner. They purveyed the best turtle soup redolent of the best sherry, the plumpest snails swimming in parsley-green butter, the most succulent venison, and savory beef accompanied by wondrous Bordeaux. They spared no expense, patience,

or perseverance in making sure that the hand-picked foods, the service, and the liquors and wines were all up to Continental snuff.

In those houses of lush mirrors, stained glass, Baccarat crystal, potted palms, and peacock feathers, New Yorkers were sinking their teeth into culinary triumphs that French chefs had pirated out of Paris, and popping the corks of cases and cases of fine vintage French wines.

Everyone seemed to be looking for the next drink and the next cocktail party, which was the high sport of the day and born out of Café Society, a term invented in 1919 by Maury Paul, William Randolph Hearst's first Cholly Knickerbocker, who saw that the Old Guard of society had apparently disappeared and that it had been replaced by people who were running about and spending a great deal of money in night clubs and restaurants.

Young college blades, just out of war uniform, and their bobbed-haired girl friends with orchids on their shoulders trotted to the Bronx-perfumed glasses of the Biltmore Bar. Upstairs, spinach suppers were spread out as the bubbly was poured by Scott and Zelda Fitzgerald, who were heralded as the high priest and priestess of the youth cult. A rebellious and reckless "dear-heart" society was spreading its arms out all across the nation, working off nervous energy stored up during World War I and provoked by the fascination and freedom of a modern world.

But then, on January 17, 1920, the big blow fell: America was told to dry up.

The Eighteenth Amendment to the Constitution of the United States, known as the Volstead Act, set down Prohibition as the law of the land. How this unmerciful deed came about can be explained in the words of H. L. Mencken, great journalist and enemy of all puritans, who wrote that "Congress is made up eternally of petty scoundrels, pusillanimous poltroons, highly vulnerable and cowardly men; they will never risk provoking the full fire of the Anti-Saloon League."

For those who have forgotten what happened, and for those too young to know, people merely threw back their heads and laughed, gave the Bad Act a big Bronx cheer, and set out to prove that legislated morality basically stinks. With the advent of this noble experiment, "noble in intent," as President Hoover was later to label it, we were off on the biggest and longest party in history, a wild, wet, and lawless one which did not end for over thirteen years. Drinking simply went "underground," and some eighty per cent of the people eventually learned to break the law and love it. The battle of the temperance folks to reform the sensual essence of man and infringe upon his liberties brought the gurgle of hip flasks and the swilling of gin until dawn in speakeasies, wild liaisons with bootleggers and smuggled booze and "Clipper Ships," bathtub gin, exploding bottles of home-made beer and smoking stills, and the taste of wood alcohol to fifteen-year-olds. Prohibition brought bribes and corrupt officials, organized crime and gangsters, gang wars, and the rat-tat-tat of the underworld's machine guns. Successful gangsters became members of a special kind of aristocracy. Important people courted their friendship and favor; their activities and felonies, private lives and funerals, were front-page news. They seemed to be the only people in the country who weren't afraid or confused.

But most of the people who broke the law were different from "Legs" Diamond, Lucky Luciano, and Frank Costello—they were just plain "wets." Sure, there were moonshiners, bootleggers, speakeasy owners, and rum-runners, but they were not criminals—not really —they just felt a man has the right to decide whether he does or doesn't take a drink. Hundreds of these old unlawful people are today honored members of the business and civic communities. They head up philanthropies, they are trustees and patrons of the arts, and board members of institutions. It is said that during Prohibition there was not one family in New York who did not have

something to do with bootleg whisky.

Folks felt as the great attorney Clarence Darrow did when he said, "The Eighteenth Amendment is an unenforceable law and a bad law. It should be treated with contempt."

In New York in 1922, beautiful youth, the wildest of all generations, followed by their elders, who had learned that liquor would take the place of young blood, screamed "Boop-Boop-a-Doop" to Sicilians as they drank their way through thirty-two thousand speakeasies, or more than double the number of legal drinking places that had existed prior to Prohibition. Typical speak owners were waiters and cooks who came together and opened a "room." They were often Sicilian- or Greek-born sailors who had jumped ship in America to avoid military conscription in their own country, then hidden out and joined the restaurant labor force. Frightened of the police, to whom they could neither account for themselves nor communicate in English, they were easy prey for gangs and Revenue men to move in on for "protection" and payoffs. All too often their speaks served rotgut booze (booze was the word for all liquor during Prohibition) which made the victim feel as if he'd been

The Jazz Age: getting blotto, plastered, and potted

3

drawn through a keyhole, or else they served decent stuff that was shamefully watered. Speakeasies of the lowest operative level just doled out wood alcohol, which could cause a man to open his eyes two minutes later and say, "Oh my God, can I see?" Some people just expired on the spot. Dank back rooms smelling like a cross between a brewery and a glue factory, these speaks made going out for a sociable drink less than a scintillating experience. But there was not much choice.

At least not until two college kids tossed their hats into the illicit drinking ring. They were John Carl Kriendler and his cousin Charles A. Berns, who put down their schoolbooks and started a series of speakeasies that would eventually culminate in the famous "21." Neither of the young men started out knowing much more than the difference between Scotch and gin, but they saw a big chance to make money. Most important, they were fed up with being poor.

Jack, born in Austria, had come to the United States with his parents when he was two years old, and his family settled in a solidly Jewish ghetto on the Lower East Side of Manhattan. Charlie's parents had migrated from the same area in Austria just before the turn of the century and moved to the immigrant-crowded West Side just above Hell's Kitchen. Jack, twenty-four and a Fordham University student who wanted to be a pharmacist, and Charlie, twenty-two, a new graduate of New York University School of Commerce with plans for law school, had both gone to night school by working as salesmen and handymen for Jack's uncle, Sam Brenner, who owned both a shoe store and a popular saloon-cum-speakeasy on opposite corners of Essex and Rivington Streets.

One day when the boys were lazing around Greenwich Village, Jack startled the more conservative Charlie by suggesting out of the blue that they go into the speak business, just until they made enough money to go back to school.

Charlie was a little dubious, but Jack, without a dime in his pocket, and persuasive character that he was, borrowed a thousand dollars, the life's savings of his sister and brother-in-law, Anna and Henry Tannenbaum, and went into business with young Edward ("Eddie") Irving. As a result of a bad debt from a young friend in the Village, Eddie had suddenly found himself with a "tea room," a tiny shop that was a cross between a peasant-type store and a coffee shop, and he needed a partner to run the place while he worked days on Wall Street. Jack and Eddie called their place the "Red Head," after the Anita Loos–type redhead silhouettes on the parchment shades of the dingy wall sconces which barely shed light on the room with its yellowed, embossed-tin walls, a lazily revolving ceiling fan, some small wooden tables, and straight-backed wooden chairs. A curtained-off alcove hid a tiny kitchen, and faded cretonne covered the front windows. Located at street level on the west side of Sixth Avenue between Fourth Street and Washington Place, the tea room stood in the shadow of the old Sixth Avenue El. On that site today, and carrying on the tradition and spirit of the venerable Red Head, stands McBell's, a favorite watering hole for the off-Broadway theater crowd.

As Pete Kriendler, Jack's younger brother, remembers the place today, "It caught on as a college hangout, and also a spot for artists, musicians, writers, newspapermen, and sportsmen who liked the atmosphere. It wasn't the usual speak where people silently packed down the hooch. Jack ran the Red Head like a fraternity room . . . a jivey, jazzy place, good clean fun—everyone dancing the Charleston, playing practical jokes, and shouting 'Nerts to you.' When the band took a break or on its days off, the customers themselves picked up the beat on the club's piano, banjoes, and drums. It was nondescript, a room to pack into and to smoke, dance, talk, and drink in.

"I used to hang around," Pete continues, "to sip a Coke—all evening. I was just sixteen, and trying to act big cheese and to dance with the flappers who came in, nice girls from uptown, the boarding-school types, who thought it was the cat's meow to paint their faces and take the El or the double-decker Fifth Avenue bus downtown to roam the Village tea rooms and speaks, without guys to escort them."

When the club got rolling, Jack pulled Charlie into the business, first as an accountant at twenty-five dollars a week, and then, when Charlie got interested in the profits to be made, as a full partner. Soon they bought out Eddie Irving, who says, "I wanted nothing to do with liquor since I was a Wall Street man." Mark Hellinger worked as the cashier, and it's said that he later wrote in his column in the *Daily News* that the Red Head was the happiest time of his life because he just sat and took cash—fifty-cent cover charges—and pocketed as much as he wanted. Jack sold booze in little dollar-an-ounce flasks, kept hidden in overcoat pockets in the coatroom, and people drank the stuff from tea cups—with orange or grape juice or ginger ale—which gave the name "cup joints" to such places.

Jack had trustworthy liquor sources in Uncle Sam Brenner and, of all people, his mother. Local bootleggers who supplied Sam delivered to Mama on East Fourth Street, and when the Red Head ran out of supplies Jack sent a message over to his mother, who filled flasks, bundled them up, and sent out the shipment in care of his little brothers, Pete, Mac, and Bob, who trundled the precious cargo westward across town in a little red wagon with groceries on the top.

Shortly after the Red Head grew popular and started making money, the boys were visited by Linkey ("The Killer") Mitchell and his cronies. They were members of a local gang known as the Hudson Dusters, a small but famous and violent all-Irish gang

made up of dockers from the West Side around Twelfth Street. It had always concentrated on gang wars, skirmishes, and gangster antics well known in New York in the early part of the century. Now the gang, like others around town, was getting into the bootleg business to offer not only bottled happiness but "protective services" as well. They wanted a part of the Red Head, but Jack and Charlie refused to talk to them. The gang repeated its approaches but to no avail. Finally, one night when Jack and Charlie were on their way home, a couple of them jumped the boys and tried to dust them up, but it was the Dusters who got creamed. A second time the gang attacked, but they took the same pummeling from Jack and Charlie.

Then one hot day, Linkey himself came through the open door of the Red Head. Taking a quick look around the room, he opened the icebox door, took out his pistol, and fired away at the ice until he got a chip that would fit in a glass. Jack and Charlie only laughed, and finally the chagrined Linkey gave up and simply took to the street, leaned against a lamp post, and shouted "Fairy, fairy" to guys

going into the club in their summertime jackets and ties.

Jack and Charlie came from tough neighborhoods and obviously could account for themselves. As Jerry Berns remembers his brother Charlie: "He would handle himself damn well. He was powerful and strong—robust as a boy and broad and hard as a man. He used to work as a blacksmith's helper when he was in his teens and he sold newspapers on the corner where he lived, at Fifty-fifth Street and Eighth Avenue. Our father was a tinsmith, and though he provided for our basic needs, for myself and my mother, my three sisters, Ann, Bea, and 'Toots,' there was nothing left over. How we got along, I don't know."

As Pete Kriendler remembers the Kriendler boys' childhood: "We spoke Yiddish almost as much as English, and we were a tough lot then . . . we would come home from a street fight minus a tooth, or clump of hair, but Mama would remind us 'They can't take away what you've got in your head.' Mama was a midwife, and she delivered over three thousand babies. That was all the income we

Carl and Sadie Kriendler, Jewish immigrants who helped settle New York's Lower East Side

had except for Jack's help after my father, a welder in the Brooklyn Navy Yard, died in the 1917 flu epidemic. We would go out on the street and steal what we could, such as a pair of roller skates from Segal-Cooper, the department store on Sixth Avenue and Eighteenth Street. Settlement houses and neighborhood clubs were the only places we—my three brothers and four sisters and myself—had to play. The tenement in which we were all raised is still standing."

In 1924 Jack and Charlie had their first serious lesson in the dangers of running a speakeasy. It was a whoopee Saturday night, the music was deafening, and the club was

Uncle Sam Brenner. At right,
Washington Square in the twenties

packed. Everyone was too busy to notice that Charlie, who was acting as screener and bouncer, was involved in a scuffle with someone at the door, and before anybody knew what happened, there was Charlie lying at the door with his throat cut ear to ear. Luckily, the cut missed the jugular, and Charlie was patched up in St. Vincent's Hospital, but he carried the scar until he died. His attacker was not a gangster but a free-loading local fireman. He had always balked at paying his bill, expecting everything to be on the house, and that night, after too many flasks and Charlie's insistence that he pay, he drew a razor.

As Charlie said later, "Sure, you had to be brave to run a speak, but give it up because of a corrupt official? No . . . the fireman angered us more than anything else. We realized that if we wanted to stay in the business and in one piece, we had to get ourselves some protection." Some young clients of theirs who were in a powerful Lower East Side Democratic organization knew the district police captain and told him that Jack and Charlie were good guys, that they ran one of the few clean shops around, no bookmaking, no gambling, no hookers, no drugs, just good booze and fun, and that they needed protection. The captain saw the boys and said, "Why didn't you tell me about these troubles? I'll see what I can do."

Jack and Charlie weren't bothered again the entire time they operated in the Village. In return for this protection, they greased the palms of the department. Of the relationship, Charlie said, "It wasn't a shakedown, just a nice, friendly arrangement. We would slip the captain a fifty-dollar bill and give out boxes of cigars to the cops on the beat. And all of them could count on the Red Head at Christmas, and free drinks and food whenever they stopped into the club."

When Jack took over the Red Head, he stopped the boring mashed-potato meal service typical of tea rooms, a low-profit opera-

tion compared to liquor, and simply served good sandwiches: "Ham *or* cheese, or ham *and* cheese." This constituted the total menu except on weekends, when the kitchen served steak and eggs.

Although the "fix" that Jack and Charlie paid to the local police wasn't much, many speak owners thought that the Red Head must be paying out gold, because the two most famous Prohibition agents in New York history, Izzy Einstein and his fat—about a quarter of a ton—partner, Moe Smith, or just "Izzy and Moe" as they were known, used to while away their time in the Red Head and never padlocked it; yet their record tallied up five thousand arrests. Izzie and Moe made pinches by masquerading as everyone from gravediggers in total exhaustion from digging and in need of a drink, to musicians, lawyers, counts, football players, and fruit vendors. The reason they never closed up the Red Head was very simple: Moe, also of Aus-

trian descent, ran a cigar store and boxing club down on the Lower East Side, and he knew the little Kriendler boys who used to hang around for an occasional free lesson.

The Red Head was in the Charles Street Police Precinct and as a result had to close at 1:00 a.m., whereas speaks on the east side of Sixth, in the Mercer Street Precinct, could stay open until as late as the clubs wanted. The precincts were like little villages unto themselves, ruled not by law but by what the police captains thought would keep their areas "clean."

Jack wanted a late-night place, a fancier club with a closed-door policy, so early in 1925 the boys closed up shop, spread their wings across the street to the southeast corner of Sixth Avenue and Washington Place, where they had bought a small establishment called the Frontón for three thousand dollars.

Only a year and a half was left on the Frontón lease, so Jack and Charlie went to see their old friend and former partner Eddie Irving, who had connections to a local alderman by the name of McAuliffe, who was in turn a right hand of a leader of Tammany Hall. As Irving recalls, "A five-year extension was secured on the lease, and through McAuliffe the boys were introduced to the chief inspector of police at the Mercer Street Precinct." The inspector was, as Irving recalls, "a big, red-haired Irishman, about two hundred and fifty pounds, with a sweet, freckled face and a desire for a drink as strong as any man's. When Alderman McAuliffe said that Jack and Charlie wanted to open a place on the Mercer side of Sixth and would sell booze, the inspector said, 'Okay, but if I catch you giving one damn nickel to any cop—federal or otherwise—I'll close you up myself.'"

Author and playwright Anita Loos.
Far left, New York where the Kriendlers lived: no bananas but plenty of rye bread, pastrami, chicken livers, and new green pickles

2

Speak Softly...
Speakeasy

There was only one thing that distinguished the basement facade of Number 88 Washington Place from others along the street—all of them dingy, below-ground-level walls with windows painted over with coal dust from the years, or boarded up to keep out the kids and cats. On the wooden steps leading down to the cellar was a bright new sisal rug running smack up to an old wooden door. Inside was the Frontón, Jack and Charlie's new speakeasy. Bright and stylized as a designer's stage set, the instant décor, typical of speaks, was *à la Español*, appropriately fitting the Spanish name *frontón*, meaning the main wall of a jai alai court.

One big room seated about sixty people, and there were twelve banquette seats and several tables with high-backed, dark, wooden chairs. The concrete floor was painted burgundy, and there were white rough stucco walls snuggling up to a low, dark-beamed ceiling with soft lighting. Red-orange-yellow-and-black-striped cloth poked out here and there in the room to partition off intimate corners and conceal the club's proudest possession: two wooden sawhorses supporting planks over a floor drain. This was the bar, and on it sat four pitchers filled with Scotch, rye, gin, and bourbon. "The point was," as Charlie once recalled, "if any trouble came, we could quickly pour the pitchers down the drain and scoot out the back through the coal cellar door and out onto Sixth Avenue."

This was a *real* speak, complete with a peep hole—the "Joe sent me" symbol of speakeasy days—and Bill Hardey, Charlie's cousin, came to help run it. He was only one of a swelling number of relatives who would, over the years, join Jack and Charlie's busi-

13

ness and their heirs' club—eventually giving "21," as one relative puts it, a tribal bond that would have abashed the Medicis.

As Bill recalls the door setup: "We had a warning button on the sidewalk railing. If someone unfamiliar came to call and insisted upon entering, one of us would run out the cellar door and around the corner and look him over. If we suspected a Revenue agent with a search warrant, the button would be pressed and the buzzer would go off inside, sending everyone scurrying to clear the pitchers, 'bottom up' the drinks, and scoot out the back door. We used to play practical jokes on one another by sneaking out and setting off the alarm."

Hardey was a "hoofer," an exhibition dancer, and in patent-leather shoes, black-string tie, ice-cream pants, and a personality as lively and daring as they come, he took charge of the club's weekend entertainment. He hired four dance-hall girls to entertain and also act as hostesses, dancing with customers and making extra money in tips. There was a five-piece band that backed up Flame Moore, a torrid torch songstress, and pianist Al Segal, a great jazz musician and the real drawing card for the club, who later coached such performers as Ethel Merman. This lineup, as Bill recalls, cost some fifty dollars a weekend.

The summer before Jack and Charlie moved to the Frontón, they went into a side business with Bill in a dance-hall venture in Harrisburg, Pennsylvania. But it flopped so miserably that Harrisburg became a word to make the boys cringe, and taught them that they weren't the business geniuses they thought they were. To compensate for their losses, and satisfy their enterprising natures and bent egos, they took over the rowboat concession at Grossinger's in the Catskill Mountains, adding newspapers, sandwiches, horse-renting, and of course liquor. This last item turned some handsome profits for not only the house, but also for the boys, and

they cemented invaluable friendships with the Grossinger Clan, who proved helpful over the years with business advice and an exchange of clients.

Up in the country, Jack and Charlie learned to ride horses and began to dance. As Bill said, "They were the clumsiest things you've ever seen. Jack didn't dance badly, but bowlegged Charlie danced with a reck-

less abandon, just the way he drove a car. He once borrowed a friend's car up in Connecticut and when he got down to Columbus Circle he snarled up the entire traffic ring. The cop there came over and looked at Charlie, looked at the Connecticut plate, and said, 'Mister, will you tell me how the hell you got *this* far?'"

Most of the old gang from the Red Head followed Jack and Charlie to the Frontón, but the place turned out to be different—quieter and generally more subdued than it had been across the street. To gain new customers, Jack and Charlie mailed and handed out cards saying "Congenial Hospitality, Jack and Charlie, Call SPR 0007." This was a promotional gimmick favored by many executive editor of the *World*, a man who reputedly knew everyone worth knowing in the underworld and bootleg business. But what really put the little Frontón on the popularity map was the presence of Mayor Jimmy Walker and his municipal greeter, Grover A. Whalen, the civic booster who invented the ticker-tape parade—and liked to be in the very center of each one. Both men,

Gentleman Mayor James J. Walker leads an old-fashioned parade

speaks; in fact, cards advertising where to find speaks appeared under apartment and hotel doors, on desks, in pockets, and were even thrown freely to the wind in federal buildings.

New clients in the club included the distinguished Villager Edna St. Vincent Millay and booming-voiced Herbert Bayard Swope, magnificent in their splendor—with top hats, striped trousers, frock coats, and gardenias in their buttonholes—frequented the speak together with a retinue of politicians and assorted ladies. They had been introduced to the club by Billy Seeman (later married in "21" by Walker), who had an apartment above the Frontón. Upon discovering it, Seeman made it his second home and moved his parties, including the mayor's coterie, from upstairs to downstairs with cases of champagne and gin and Cuban *Carta Oro* rum. Seeman, known as one of the best party-givers of several decades, was a man who firmly believed that "whisky kills all germs." If one wanted to live long, then drink up—a philosophy that certainly worked for *him*. It is said that he started the day with a glass of gin and did a soft-shoe in "21" when he had

reached an age when "they should," as one friend said, "have had an ambulance waiting outside."

The Frontón policy was to stay open and capture business as long as anyone was left breathing, which meant that the club, which didn't fill up and start swinging until about 11:00 p.m., was often open until the middle of the morning, particularly on weekends. By hiring an Italian chef and starting a little kitchen operation—specializing in steaks, chops, sauced meats, and fancy sandwiches—Jack and Charlie made a bid for those who liked to dine as well as drink. Word soon spread that they had honest food, better than the average speak around town, and the

club became known as "The Little Restaurant." With almost childlike interest, Jack became fascinated with the cooking pots, and would poke about trying to help the chef. As Harold Alpert, who has been the carpet supplier for Jack and Charlie and "21" for forty-six years now, said, "The chef did okay, but Jack's *real* contribution came when rain leaked into the little kitchen area from glass reflector plates set in steel frames in the sidewalk above. Then Jack would stand by the range holding a tarpaulin over the chef and food."

Adding wines, which came through an Italian bootlegger who took them off ships docked out in the Hudson, Jack cast himself in the role of spiffy speakeasy restaurateur, sometimes to the point of overdressing the part. One day when some boots were in the club talking to Charlie, Jack came in with a flower in his buttonhole and a jazzy pin-striped suit. "Who's that?" one of the booties said to Charlie. "Oh, that's my cousin," Charlie said. "What's he, a floorwalker?" returned the boot.

By the mid-twenties, competition had grown keen in the speakeasy business, and there were, by one estimate, some one hundred thousand speaks in town, or one for every fifty-six people (booze was also available from the local fruit vendor, drugstore, hardware shop, hairdresser, shoeshine parlor, and even the mailman and one's maid). But Jack and Charlie flourished because they offered an honest *boîte* with trustable liquor and decent food. Only people of a particular genre were allowed in, so it had none of the homogenized society found in other speaks—one midtown place reported elbow-rubbing by such people as Lord and Lady Mountbatten, evangelist Aimee Semple McPherson,

At left, Billy Seeman. At right, Grover A. Whalen, New York's official host to visiting celebrities, sits next to waving Howard Hughes and Albert I. Lodwich in a triumphal ride down Broadway

great madam Polly Adler, and visitor to the city Al Capone—some crowd. A man could take his girl friend or wife into the Frontón and have a good time without clinking unwashed glasses with gangsters, their molls, or guys who wanted to uproot a lamp post or punch a cop.

School had been forgotten by Jack, who would never graduate. But Charlie, determined and persevering, had diligently kept at his studies by going to school during the day and working full time in the club at night. "I slept by grabbing quick catnaps here and there, practically learning to sleep standing on my feet," he once said, "but a sharp business discipline comes with a schedule that is almost impossible—you budget time, concentrate energies, and pool resources." In 1925 he took his bar exam, cheered on by Village neighbors, even the chief inspector of police, who came into the club to celebrate when Charlie passed with flying colors and became a lawyer at last.

Invaluable friendships had been made with both the local police and the fire brigade, there being, as Charlie said, "just proper thanks on both sides." The local fire chief used to love to come into the club with his wife when he was off duty to have a few snorts and dance a little. He was never charged. One day during a hard rain the sewers rushed up through the toilets and the chief called his crew and pumped the club dry.

Shortly after that a flash fire occurred. Everyone cleared out, including Jack and Charlie, who first poured pitchers, called the fire department, then grabbed suitcases with business records, extra bottles, and a card index file of customers' names and addresses—their "traveling business"—and disappeared through the back door. They went around to Dave's Blue Room Deli across the street from the club and watched the blaze. The fire chief finally arrived and spotted the partners, went over to them, and said with a wink and nudge, "We've wrecked the place, think of all the money you'll get from the insurance." Jack and Charlie paled and moaned, "We're not insured, we're a speak!" The chief paused, then said, "We'll fix it up for you." They did.

All the time that Jack and Charlie operated in the Village they were never raided, but Revenue agents gave constant torment to many of their speak neighbors who did not know how to negotiate or could not speak English well enough to make a deal. They

Coast Guard capture off Shinnecock, Long Island: $220,000 worth of liquor from a rum-runner

would call Jack and Charlie to speak for them, and the boys made it a profitable arrangement three ways: the agent got his pay-off; the owner was not called up on a felony charge; and Jack and Charlie were left alone because the agents made enough money on the others.

In 1926 the happy little Frontón came to an abrupt end when the city of New York started condemnation proceedings against property in the area of Washington Place and Sixth Avenue to build a subway station for the Independent line. An Italian bootlegger friend advised Jack and Charlie to move up to midtown Manhattan where the speakeasy business was beginning to concentrate. The Red Head and Frontón behind them, they decided to take the big jump and try the big time, uptown.

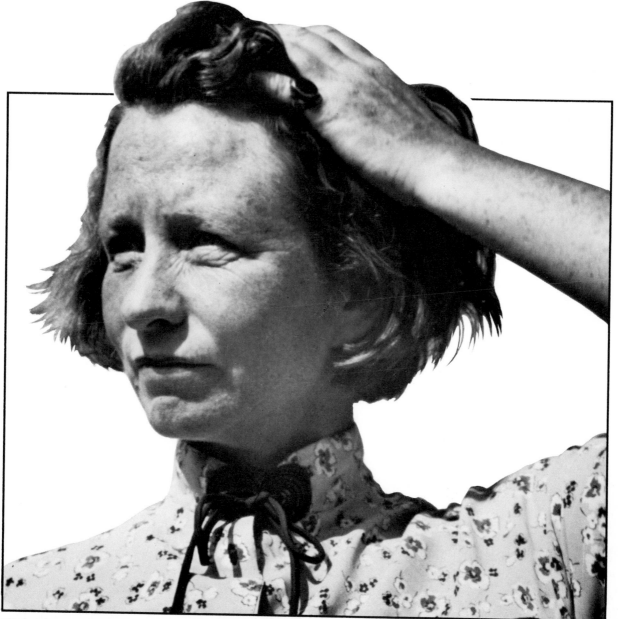

1922 Pulitzer Prize—winner Edna St. Vincent Millay

3

This Could Be
the Start
of Something Big

Could two young boys from tenement life who slept on fire escapes in the summertime to keep cool, and huddled around cooking pots in the wintertime to keep warm, find happiness in a big city townhouse in the midst of filthy-rich midtown Manhattan of 1926? "Let's try it," Jack said as he stood with key poised before the iron gate in front of 42 West Forty-ninth Street. Jack and Charlie's new speakeasy was in a fashionable townhouse in the heart of the carriage-trade residential area, just a few doors from where Bergdorf Goodman then stood on Fifth Avenue and Forty-ninth.

Set upon a Columbia University leasehold (Columbia still owns the property between Forty-eighth and Fifty-first streets from Fifth to Sixth Avenues), No. 42, once owned by Albert H. Wiggin, later chairman of the board of The Chase National Bank, had been leased to Martin Quinn, Sr., head of the stock-exchange firm of E. C. Benedict & Co. Quinn terminated his lease in 1925, leaving because the street had been rezoned for commercial rentals and the new speakeasies made Forty-ninth a very noisy area at night. Caesar Betti and Peter Mossi then opened a restaurant and "ran a little liquor" in No. 42, but the business never really got off the ground. They wanted out just as Jack and Charlie were being forced to leave the Frontón. Negotiations to move uptown took place through Betti's attorney, Julius Hallheimer, who had been a patron of the Frontón. Within one day, Jack and Charlie had their new speak complete with furnishings and cellar stock for a price of fifteen thousand dollars, having put up their entire savings of five thousand dollars in cash and given Betti a mortgage for ten thousand dollars.

They christened No. 42 "The Puncheon

Jack

Grotto," though the boys also came to call it the "Puncheon," the "Grotto," "No. 42," or, a time when speaks were usually just "Harry's" or "Joe's," just "Jack and Charlie's." Charlie explained that the reason for so many different names was to avoid evidence of business continuity. The Internal Revenue Service looked for returns from the name of a place, not an address.

But the fondest nickname for No. 42, at least for its contingent of Yale clients, was "Ben Quinn's Kitchen." Yale man Quinn, the son of Martin, Sr., tells the story: "I first went to Jack and Charlie's in the spring of 1926. A friend told me it was an attractive new speakeasy with good liquor, so we hopped in a taxi and my friend gave an address that I didn't hear. We arrived at a New York basement stoop-house with an iron gate, stepping down three steps and then up two. Admitted by a doorman, we tossed our coats on a banquette, went up three more steps, and turned to the left through a small door and then down two steps into a room where we found small tables covered with red-and-white plaid tablecloths and a small bar at the far end to the right. The moment I entered the room I knew it was my old laundry. I was sure because my feet were so accustomed to the small flights of steps up and down, which I had traversed so many times in the dark upon returning home at night and to get a glass of milk from the icebox, just beyond the laundry. 'I was born in this house,' I shouted upon my discovery. 'This is my old home. Martinis for everyone!'"

Quinn "made this place a habit of Yale men—and quite a good habit," wrote the *Yale Record*. The article continued, "It is a genuine pleasure to find such as the Puncheon . . . the watering-place of particular epicures—you may mingle with them there in the expensive aroma of good cigars. Jack makes it a pleasure to stop singing and be quietly respectable, while Charlie compels you to remain in a good humor . . . cuisine comes first to both of them—you are expected to enjoy eating and you may drink if you wish. Familiar faces will always be present . . ."

Humorist and critic Robert Benchley quickly adopted the Puncheon as his hangout, bringing with him such Algonquin Round Table regulars as Alexander Woollcott, Franklin P. Adams, Edna Ferber, and Dorothy Parker.

Jack's dream was to give his speakeasy the ease and elegance of a European coffeehouse with the overtone of an eighteenth-century English pub, a "Sam Johnson place" where men of letters and of social position could come at any time, under any excuse, to simply exchange ideas and chat, have business conferences, meet friends, read newspapers and pick up messages, sit long and freely over drinks, and entertain wives and girl friends. Jack went for broke and hired Henri Geib, an Alsatian, who had at one time been chef to Kaiser Wilhelm II. Geib, an exceptionally brilliant food man, established a kitchen in the finest Continental tradition and stayed with Jack and Charlie until 1939, when he retired. (Later he came out of retirement to become personal luncheon chef to cosmetic king Charles Revson, who supposedly used to go into "21" and other places about town straight from his plant with his hands stained red from testing cosmetics.)

No one was permitted in the Puncheon who wasn't known to the house, personally introduced by a regular, or looked like the type that Jack hoped to attract. During this early period, the Yalies and literary people kept the club alive, but it became clear that more traffic was needed to help support the mortgage payments. Jack was reluctant to lower his standards, but Charlie, who had been tending the peep hole assisted by Jack's younger brother Mac (Maxwell), convinced Jack to be more lenient. Bill Hardey, who had come uptown with the boys and took over management of the bar, helped by

. . . and Charlie

23

Bootlegger's Packard and booze confiscated in 1922. Right, Dorothy Parker and husband, Alan Campbell

bringing in a gaggle of dance-hall girls who drew men into the club. Small comfort to the discriminating Jack. Happily then, the social and famous started to ring the Puncheon's bell.

Prohibition had closed New York's great bars and wining and dining houses, and elegant and erudite New Yorkers had found it difficult to suddenly stomach "speak spaghet" and "New Jersey Bordeaux," so it was natural that the discriminating would be seduced by pasta to a wickedly beautiful level: spaghetti served with a lush tomato-and-black-truffle sauce, a rich and gastronomically salacious dish.

The Puncheon was not inexpensive. As a regular of the house, Herbert ("Herby") Rubsamen, remembers, lunch for two could set one back twenty dollars. "In fact," he says, "nothing was cheap in those days . . . a bottle of champagne was twenty-two dollars and so was a pair of shoes from Brooks

an offering of French wines, champagnes and cognacs, and a menu that sported such delicate foods as fresh crab and brook trout, prosciutto, petite marmite Henry IV, bouillabaisse, plump omelettes oozing with a purée of mushrooms and enhanced with mornay sauce and a truffle julienne, saddle of lamb, roast veal, and filet mignon. All this topped off with pâtisserie and real Viennese coffee with thick whipped cream. Jack also competed successfully with the pasta circuit by having the chef perfect a lip-smacking dish that was certainly unique and elevated Brothers. And an evening out? I recall in 1926 when I invited five people to dinner, Dick Buck, Beatrice Bixby, Thelma and Bernice Chrysler, and my brother Ernest. We all met for dinner at the Puncheon Grotto, after which we went to a musical comedy, then back to the Puncheon for a brandy. Then we went on to the Club Richmond, where George and Julie Murphy were dancing. We closed the place up and wound up at Reubens for breakfast. My brother later thanked me for paying the six-hundred-and-twenty-five-dollar tab."

Lady with a good "belt"

Once the Puncheon took hold, Jack set about the serious task of being the front man in the business, spending sixteen hours a day developing the character of the place, catering to comforts, wants, and whims of his patrons, and psyching out their eccentricities—treating each as an individual. Jack was evolving into a dandy despot, a Napoleon of the restaurant business, and he became increasingly determined not only to have Café Society as customers but also to move into its ranks himself.

Charlie, on the other hand, was moderate, slow, and deliberate; he carefully considered all business decisions, pulling no punches or pretenses. His concern was the back of the house; he was the inside man who sat back and quietly dined on club sandwiches while he made certain that the books balanced in the black. They made quite a pair: What Jack didn't know, Charlie did. It was evident that their talents balanced perfectly and that they moved more effectively together than separately. Charlie once said, "Jack supplied looks and charm, while I supplied only brains."

Lawyer Charlie coped with the buying, handling, and storing of liquor and wine, and

26

Federal agents smashing kegs of bootlegged beer

dealt with Federal Revenue agents and the police. Shortly after the move to Forty-ninth Street, the police precinct captain came to call, explaining that to protect himself he had to make a friendly arrest—to put it on the record that the club sold liquor. Charlie was told to put out two bottles, that a policeman would pick them up, and that the boys would be booked but would go free on bail. Which is exactly what happened. The local police were usually sympathetic "wets," partly because they were drinkers but also for the payoffs they took from the speak owners. But from time to time it was necessary to come up with a "good show" for the city's Prohibition commissioner.

Some clubs paid protection money to bootleggers, some to Federal agents, and others to the local police, who were at that time the brunt of many a joke. One memorable story has it that a local paper one day printed this item: "Finnegan has been appointed to the defective force of this city." The police complained, and the paper printed a correction saying "Finnegan has been appointed to the detective farce of this city."

The Federal agents were not as friendly as the local police, and many were real

shakedown artists, particularly the group that worked the neighborhood around the Puncheon. They were young men of good families who saw a way to pick up some easy money by joining the Prohibition unit. To handle this, a group of speaks in the Puncheon area created an organization headed by John Perona of The Bath Club, who later founded El Morocco. He was negotiator for the group, and when one of the Federal agents would come around to a speak, the owner would simply send him to Perona for his payoff. All in all, it rarely cost any one speak more than a thousand dollars a year, in addition to a few free meals and drinks along the way.

There was one serious raid at the Puncheon in 1927. As Charlie once remembered it: "The raid was ordered personally by

Left, salvaging liquor from a rum-runner. Below, exporter Roddie Williams. Right, the rum-runner *Linwood* set afire to avoid capture by a Coast Guard patrol boat

Mabel Walker Willebrandt, Assistant Attorney General in charge of Prohibition enforcement. Two things had put her on our trail. First, the rumor that we were the only New York speakeasy in continuous operation that had never been raided. Secondly, a valued customer, a Southern gentleman, who didn't trust his local brew, telephoned to ask us to send him some of our whisky. The employee who took the call stupidly sent it through the mail with the return address on the package. The Post Office spotted it, reported it, and this made Mrs. Willebrandt doubly determined to get us. Selling liquor through the mail was an onerous offense. Though the case was long and drawn out, Julius Hallheimer, who had become our attorney, squared us off with a plea of guilty of possession of liquor. We paid a fine and that was that."

Ironically, the raid turned out to be great advertising for the boys. The papers reported that the liquor confiscated at the club and analyzed by Federal chemists was of the finest quality. A newspaper asked, "Why raid a place that is serving good liquor and not poisoning anybody?"

But as Charlie added, "The raid taught us

to be more discreet about our liquor storage, which had previously been stashed around under the tables and chairs and in closets. It seems that the brownstone next to us was occupied on the first two floors only, so we crawled out on the roof and through the skylight into the next house, where we stored all our liquor. When Hallheimer found out about our being 'squatters' there, he had a fit. The owner next door could have been nailed. Luckily, no one ever found our cache."

Many tales have been told about where Jack and Charlie's rum came from during those supposedly dry days. Here's the straight story from an ex-bootlegger, Murray (not his real name but he prefers anonymity). He helped supply the boys, and he seemed to revel in recalling the olden days.

"'Hello there, you've got partners,' the gangsters would say to me, poking a gun in my head and snarling, 'We've got to eat, too.'

"Sure it was dangerous," he explained. "If it wasn't the Booze Busters, as we called the Prohibition unit that was set up under the Bureau of Internal Revenue, and made up of newly appointed 'deputy sheriffs' who shot

wild at anything they saw wiggle, it was the gangsters.

"In the early days of Prohibition, most booze was American 100-proof pre-1920 liquor from government warehouses, looted out by petty gangsters who sold it underground, or it was medicinal 'alcohol' sold through a doctor's Rx. A man could get a pint every ten days with a legitimate prescription if he could prove 'illness.' Many doctors sold their prescription books—theoretically controlled by the government—to druggists, and they sold Rx's to the public, advertising in newspapers that they would fill all prescriptions, and at a good price. The Longacre Pharmacy was famous for the best gin in town. People would run in, buy a pint, and down it on the run or in some public toilet. Then this got sticky . . . doctors were arrested, the liquor was oftentimes watered, or it could be wood alcohol. Counterfeiters printed fake prescription books, and the public must have forged every doctor's name in the metropolitan phone directories. Besides, there weren't enough supplies.

"So 'pulling' booze across the Canadian border started with Canadians supplying us through the Quebec Liquor Commission. I started pulling as a young guy, and a fellow paid me fifty dollars a trip to cross the border . . . drive a car on a dirt road from Lacolle, Canada, over a bridge into Champlain, New York, and then on to Plattsburg, about a forty-mile run. On my first trip, I was in a five-car caravan, going first, having drawn straws to see who would be the leader. We ran with our headlights on and then cut them off just as we hit the bridge. The first two cars got through, but the last three were gunned with shotgun blasts. Then I went into business for myself, buying a Buick, and later a big Packard touring car with window curtains and the springs strengthened to take the liquor load.

"A car would hold about twenty cases . . .

bottles stacked neck to neck; they came wrapped separately in paper, so they were easy to store in the back seat. Some pullers had cars with fake paneling and tin racks under the floor boards. We called them 'chickens.' In those early days, we'd buy at about fifty dollars a case in Canada and sell it for about a hundred dollars in New York. I also had contacts with farmers whose land straddled the Canadian-American line, and I'd pull into their barns, load up, and shoot right back to the city. I drove back and forth so much I knew the roads by heart. Sometimes we brought beer down in potato sacks, but most of the supply came from city breweries operating with paid police protection. Then came a switch: the local-yokel gangsters, just farmers and smalltowners, started sticking us up. We could never travel alone but always in caravans over the Adirondacks. I had an Italian who 'rode shotgun' with me —a 12-gauge pointed out the right window. When I'd get back to New York, I'd drop off my load with Jack and Charlie, who waited for me to arrive in the middle of the night.

"If you were caught at the border, you were fined and put out on bail, and your vehicle confiscated. No one ever went back for a hearing, he'd just forfeit bail money, car, and cargo; but some guys went to public auctions to buy back their motor cars. Supplies were also taken off transatlantic liners anchored in the Hudson. Jack and Charlie had fellows who worked the docks—I didn't —and they took dozens of cases of liquor and wines at a time off the steamships with the cooperation of the crews. During dry days, these ships were the scene of great private parties since they were 'neutral territory,' and sailing the Atlantic became a real hobby.

"One of the unusual booties I knew who supplied for the Puncheon was a loner called 'Whitey'—no one knew any other name for him. He took small lots of bottles off steamers by hiding them in his overcoat, a big thing that swept down to the ground and had rows and rows of pockets inside. He would walk off a boat loaded with booze and go straight to No. 42 and into the coatroom, where he unloaded his pockets, then go back to the ships for more, making many trips across town each day. Two guys named O'Connor and Donahue also helped supply the Puncheon, and they worked by delivering in a hearse. No one knew where these Irishmen got their supply, but it was good stuff.

"The second era of bootlegging brought hordes of supplies from 'Rum Row' boats, anchored off the New Jersey and Long Island coasts. This dried up Canadian pulling, started the expression 'right off the boat,' and the prices were cut about half all the way around. Ships loaded up in Bermuda or in the Bahamas and nearby islands would anchor outside the three-mile limit. We would speed out in fast boats, load up the 'rum,' and shoot back to shore where we'd unload at caretakers' cottages on Long Island estates . . . they were in the business with us. We'd carry some four thousand dollars in cash a trip in a shoe, going out with fishermen we'd hire who were oftentimes known to take a boot's money and throw him to the fish. The best bet was to run your own boat.

"Genuine liquor—pure stuff opposed to the watered bottles the ships usually sold— was called the 'Real McCoy,' an expression supposedly stemming from Captain William ('King Rum-Runner') McCoy, of the schooners *Arethusa* and *Tomoka*, among many he ran, who carried pure, real booze. He could carry fifteen hundred cases in the hold. Without boxes but with the booze bagged in ham sacks, she would carry two thousand cases. Then in 1924 a twelve-mile legal limit of American territorial waters was set, and the ships simply anchored beyond U.S. Coast Guard jurisdiction. This distance drove off a lot of small boats—too far out in the sea—and the gangsters made a business of bringing booze to the shore in bigger boats. Then they began to hijack the Rum Row ships. Shooting-and-killing battles went on out over the sea.

"The British government closed up the Bahamas trade—prompted by our government's pushing—and the ships came supplied from Saint Pierre and Miquelon, French islands off the coast of Newfoundland. We never had trouble on our land transportations, but the gangsters used to hijack one another, and their loaded trucks were preceded and followed on the highways by armed cars. God-awful battles sometimes raged, just as if a war was going on.

"When the rum-running got big, crime got going. We had legitimate 'buying offices' for selling booze, with printed lists we would show to clients like Jack and Charlie. A lot of boots sold bathtub quality, with faked labels, but I sold only good stuff. When my office got big, the underworld moved in on me. That wasn't an easy situation—friends of mine got killed. Some gangsters had their own offices, like Abner ("Longy") Zwillman, out of New Jersey, who, it's rumored, won his reputation by walking into a speakeasy in Newark and shooting another gangster in the testicles.

"Jack and Charlie never bought from the syndicates, but always from 'freelancers' like myself who sold higher but were safer all the way around. I used to hang around the Puncheon, and also later in '21' . . . we were all good friends."

When Murray, now in his eighties and spry as a spring chicken, was asked why he got into the bootlegging business, he shrugged, and then his eyes misted over while he literally licked his chops and said, "Adventure, that was a romantic and exciting era for young people. And fifty dollars then was like fifty thousand dollars to me now. Jack and Charlie felt the same way . . . we all felt that way."

From the outside No. 42 was anything but imposing, but inside Jack and Charlie's speakeasy the famous and picturesque of New York were drinking barrels and barrels of spirits, mixed into gin rickeys, Bronxes, orange blossoms, daiquiris, Bacardis, pink ladies, whisky sours, martinis, and side cars —the drinks destined to go down in history as "the cocktails of the twenties." Even off-limits watering of the regulars was cared for by enterprising Jack, who daily mixed up

Typical tribute to a gangster: funeral procession in Passaic, New Jersey, for underworld king Willie Moretti

fifty to one hundred bottles of cocktails and sold "pre-packaged" drinks to lunchers who carried their sundowner jollies home with them. Others rapped at the peep hole to pick up a supply, and it was not uncommon for a chauffeured Hispano-Suiza to drive up in the late afternoon and a handsome man sprint out and into the club to fetch a few bottles to take home to the drawing room. The tidy profits received from this venture, however, were not the only incentive. Townhouse

briefcase.

By 1929, people were making and spending a lot of money, and everyone seemed to be playing the stock market. "I just made twenty grand in twenty minutes" was not an uncommon remark. Money—everyone seemed to have it, and Jack and Charlie did too. Jack and Charlie were poor no more. But suddenly the picnic of material progress ended and the roaring spirit and splendiferous spending of the twenties ground to a

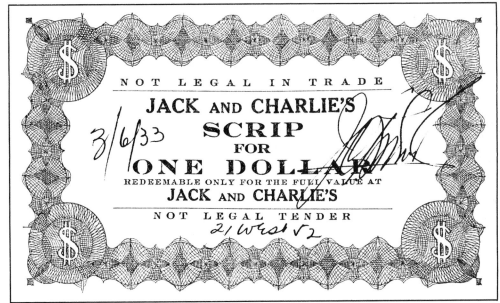

dwellers Jack and Charlie would open their club at any hour to stir up a martini for a friend to save him from a "narrow escape from death in the desert," as H. L. Mencken once described the feeling when one was "near to going dry." Mencken loved the Puncheon, and came—at any hour—to drink and to rub his caustic "wet words" about the bar, bantering his homespun Baltimore philosophy up against the city chic of Frank Crowninshield of *Vanity Fair*, the humor of Will Rogers, the financial genius of Jean Paul Getty (later to become a close friend of Jack's), the critiques of George Jean Nathan, and the antics of F. Scott Fitzgerald, who sped in and out of New York and the Puncheon with scandal in his wake and gin in his

sudden halt: Black Tuesday hit in October of 1929. Almost immediately, the Puncheon began to feel the shock of the Depression, and the boys went into conference. If anything ever brought out the business *chutzpah* of these enterprising young men, the Depression did it. Lose everything *they* had built up? Not likely. Coming out of their huddle, Charlie said, "We work for the long haul, not for the short profit." With that, and contrary to other such establishments about town, their prices held the line. Their tack was to stand by their clients by never giving anyone a headache over an unpaid bar bill, and to issue credit and advance money to club patrons who were left with no ready bar money or were just plain stranded. The club's policy was "If you want to come in, come in, you're welcome to charge." Later, as the Depression continued to hold many folks short of cash, Jack and Charlie printed their own scrip, and during the bank holiday of 1933 they advanced funds, cashed checks, and held money for such friends as Bea Lillie when she went off to England for a spell. They became known as "bankers to the royal families of New York." In fact, Ernest B. Rubsamen once recounted how, the day after the banks closed, Jack and Charlie went about the club giving out fifty-dollar bills, knowing that their patrons had no access to a bank and that many were suddenly left without enough walking-about money.

In the long run, however, Jack and Charlie lost no money—most of the checks they held were honored later and they gained life-long patronage from the people they befriended. Their generosity was not purely for business reasons alone, but grew out of a genuine sense of friendship. Years ago, when Peter Lorre filed for bankruptcy and came jauntily into the club the next day, Jack and Charlie gave him no bill and offered him use of their private car and chauffeur. Orson Welles went into the club when he was only nineteen and completely broke. The boys permitted him to sign his tabs, even for the cigars, which cost more than his monthly rent downtown in Greenwich Village. They were all family, really.

You no sooner get one problem solved than you have to go into a meeting over another . . . or so it seemed to Jack and Charlie, because, as if the Depression weren't enough, on top of that the boys found themselves homeless *again*. Civic progress forced them to bow to the Rockefeller Center project. It turned out that the Puncheon was sitting in the middle of the construction plan. For eleven thousand dollars cash and six months to find a new home, Jack and Charlie agreed to cancel out the term remaining on their lease. Now they were determined to buy their own building, and they immediately found one on East Fifty-fourth Street between Park and Lexington Avenues for a low price of some forty thousand dollars. But just at the same time, a brownstone at 21 West Fifty-second Street came available, and since they didn't want to leave their old neighborhood and police and Prohibition friends, they bought "21" from the Hochstadter family at the high price of one hundred and thirty thousand dollars.

Although many great parties were given by Jack and Charlie, none has matched the famous "demolition party" staged on New Year's Eve, December 31, 1929. This was the last night for the boys at No. 42 before they moved to No. 21—and it was probably the only time that they reached the vulgar, bilious tempo of the Prohibition era; but still they did it with style. The invitation list included a special group of favorite "trustee members" such as Robert Benchley, Gilbert Kahn, Broadway producer Alex Aarons, Bea Lillie, the Irish poet Ernest Boyd, and silent-film folks Doris Kenyon and Milton Sills. As someone said, "Who *wasn't* there is a better question." Bill Hardey remembers the party:

"We had Hawaiians with guitars strolling about as entertainment, the house served Major Baileys (mint juleps with gin), planter's punches, and sours, or your choice of drink. Bill Leeds and Ben Finney decided we should have hard-boiled eggs as an hors d'oeuvre since they bring good luck, but I substituted uncooked eggs. When everyone banged everyone else to break the shells, the party really got going.

"Charlie then handed everybody crow-bars, pickaxes, and hammers, and we began tearing the place apart to move the speak. What we didn't want to take with us we chopped to splinters, and a friendly cop on the beat [Vlav Wieghorst, who later became a famous Western painter], *riding his horse,* came inside and helped trample the rubble. A famous banker—I shan't mention his name—tore apart the men's room and wore the toilet seat around his neck while he did the hula. Doris Kenyon personally demolished the ladies' room, wearing *that* toilet seat around her neck as if it were a lavaliere. During the party, everyone tried to think of a name for the new place. Charlie simply figured that since No. 21 is half of 42, and No. 42 brought them luck, then why not just call it Jack & Charlie's '21.'

"At the end of the evening, amid choking dust and debris, and as bottles of champagne emptied over monied heads, the crowd started singing 'Auld Lang Syne.' Tears flowed. Young Mac had about as much as he could take. He got up on a chair and said, 'Why is everybody so sad? We're only moving three blocks uptown!'

"We laughed and started parading northward through the snowy streets carrying pots and pans, bottles and furnishings, and onto carts we heaped chairs and boxes of glasses and table service. At the last minute someone nostalgically said, 'Let's take the iron gate, it's part of Jack & Charlie's.' The next day the gate was up, and we were all at '21' for lunch, though we had, I might add, a real case of the awful-awfuls!"

4

The Proprietors
Make
the Myth

A barroom becomes loved, if it does, because of the stamp of its owners. It is the mood of a place more than the drinks that captures the public's fancy, and no one could have done better at creating this elusive asset than Jack and Charlie at their new speakeasy. Backed by brother Mac, now in the club full time, they set a kind of informality unlike anything that had ever been known in New York. A bootlegger friend of the house from the early days remembers the time he stepped through the iron gate, rang the golden bell on the iron-grille door, and was admitted into the small, dimly lit lobby, where, as he recalls:

"You won't believe this, but I nearly got pushed over by four men all dressed head-to-foot in black who swooped in carrying gunnysacks on their backs. They darted through the crowd with this one fellow dropping a rattling, heavy bag—obviously booze they were delivering in ham bags—on Howard Hughes's foot and another bumping the rump of a lady who was talking to another lady, who was jiggling her furs about her while she was giving Gary Cooper the eye.

"But no wonder the lobby seemed crowded, because on the floor as if it was the center stage was Mac favoring the guests with his version of

'Yippie ki-yi-o, get along little dogie,
It's your misfortune and none of my
own . . .
You know that Wyoming will be your
new home.'

"Mac always claimed that he could sing best in a prone position, though Lawrence Tibbett was the only guy we knew who ever had the courage to tell Mac frankly that his whisky voice left much to be desired *regardless* of his position. Jack, on the other hand, also a fan of the Old West, knew that cowboys sing to restless herds of grazing cattle to keep them quiet, and he let Mac perform his poignant ballads to the hungry patrons who daily scruffed up hundreds of dollars' worth of permanently stilled beef. Along with lots of booze and branch water, to be sure.

"Jack was keeping check on the lobby, and behind him trotted chuffing Mr. Spitz, his tailor, with a mouth full of pins and a pair of pants for Jack to try on. Through the whole bunch came Charlie, leading a fast-stepping chap by his tightened tie—Charlie used to employ this 'choke collar' technique to get rowdy college boys out."

While the proprietors certainly supplied the atmosphere, the club's physical décor was the creation of Frank Applegate Buchanan, an artist, engineer, and bon vivant whose original design for Jack & Charlie's has continued to grow over the years with a life of its own. Buchanan simply took the one-family townhouse No. 21—in the beginning, the club was only one-third the size it is today—and left it alone as much as possible, installing only a library-sized barroom beyond the lobby. Half of the small room was taken up with a nine-foot bar set into the northwest corner, leaving space for only about eight tables. The exclusivity of the seating was built in. With bare wood floor, beamed ceiling, plaques, and drinking signs, it had a delightfully rakish and informal air that was a direct contrast to the upstairs dining rooms with crystal chandelier, velvet, palms, and white linen in the front room, and tapestries and library-type paneling in the back room.

Not having been raised in the midst of material possessions, Jack turned to collecting—anything from Georgian silver, china, and crystal to painting and mementos, all of which he put about the house to encourage a real home atmosphere. First he bought at estate sales about town, and eventually in the

auction rooms of Europe. One of his proud finds was King Alfonso's gold-trimmed wineglasses, which were later used to serve the Duke and Duchess of Windsor, who always sent a cable to the club in advance of their New York arrival, paving the way for their royal palates. Today the Duchess says that she likes the club because it is so attractively appointed.

Daily one would find in Jack & Charlie's speakeasy hideaway—lifting bartender Bill's, Harry's, Emil's, or Gus's blood-percolating salvations—such clientpower as the social Esmond O'Brien and Ben Finney, one of the

Vanderbilts or Whitneys giving a racing tip, any number of Harvard and Yale men, and such folks about town as Eddie McIlvain, Louella Gear, Howard Dietz, Miriam Hopkins, Bernard Gimbel, and Harold Ross.

Among the beloved eccentrics who took to appearing daily was Heywood Broun, big, burly, and looking as if he slept in his clothes. Upon arrival he would go into the men's

Left, a voice of edelweiss—upright Mac.
Below, natty tailor Spitz and
Mac outside Jack & Charlie's "21"

room, take off his shirt and put it into the wastebasket, then send the men's room attendant racing up the street to buy a new one. Later in the bar he would marvel aloud that his laundry bills were exceedingly low.

Upstairs in the dining room, tended by headwaiter Philip, a colorful collection of "our people" would assemble, led by Lucius Beebe, a gourmet spokesman of the thirties and forties, a believer in the cult of Cordon Bleu, and a man who admired no one save a friend who "brushed his teeth with a light Chablis." Upon hearing that Beebe was to undergo surgery, a friend at the bar once assured the gathering, "Naturally they'll open Lucius at room temperature." Beebe pontificated on "21's" superb fare and described dining in New York once the boys appeared on the scene thus: "The turtle soup ceased to be merely a bath of hot sherry floating minuscule cubes of India rubber to prove they had liquor in the kitchen. It was no longer necessary to carry bail money when one dined out for fear of being tossed in the poky just after the fish and Chablis. Train oil and corrosive sublimate were no longer the essential ingredients of a martini, and you didn't have to get falling down drunk by ten in the morning unless you really wanted to. A feeling of stability was abroad . . . Jack & Charlie's would still be there tomorrow."

Pals like Beebe were treated to Jack's private store of Napoleon brandy, which was brought out when he whispered to Burt Walsh, who kept the liquor supplies hidden, to "fetch the private stock." This went on for a year or two until it occurred to Jack to ask how much was left. Burt said, "We haven't had any for months now." Stunned, Jack asked what the hell he and the others had been drinking, and Burt told him, "Oh, I just keep filling the Napoleon bottle with any good brandy we have in the house."

Johnny Seeman recalls that when he graduated from the coatroom to handling wines, "I didn't know whisky from 'Château Feet,' but I learned by the design of the labels." No wine lists were printed then, so that no evidence could fall into the wrong hands, but the menus were tediously written out by a French waiter in a virtually illegible blue and red script which caused customers to squint and bemoan the confusion between *poussin* and *poissons*. The spidery text in-cluded such delicacies as trout in brown butter, truffles in pastry, livers from Strasbourg, and turtle steak. Such familiar-to that-era people as Doris Duke Cromwell, Damon Runyon, Prince Serge Obolensky, and Charles Laughton came to indulge in Louis Roederer '24, generous spoons of caviar, plump oysters, snails, Sole Marguéry, rare filet, asparagus (eaten in the correct man-

ner, by picking it up by the fingers), pyramids of crackling-fragile pommes de terre soufflées (an item also eaten by hand) . . . and finish off with a refreshing macédoine de fruits au Triple Sec.

Two of the carriage-trade dishes that epitomized the flair and extravagance applied to dining in Jack & Charlie's—and typical of the thirties in New York—were canard sauvage à la presse and Steak Diane (as familiar to patrons of early "21" as Jack and Charlie themselves), both dishes prepared tableside by a captain and his crew of waiters. They are still highlights of "21's" culinary expertise, since regulars of the house know that they are available and may be ordered "off the menu," the Steak Diane anytime (associate headwaiter Walter Weiss, in the bar, is the Steak Diane expert in "21" today) and the pressed duck during mallard season as done by headwaiter Joseph Mino.

Left, Lucius Beebe pontificating on his favorite subjects: food, drink, and society. Below, the original "21" bar

Jack was extremely fussy about who came into "21," and the door was securely guarded by peep-hole receptionist Jimmie Coslove (alias Collins), the legendary "Jimmy of the front door," a trademark of "21." If he knew the caller, the door swung open, but if he didn't—sometimes even though the petitioner presented the famed yellow card with Jack's initials signaling "okay" (a number 34 on the card was Jack's code for "keep the stiff out")—the peep would invariably snap shut. Occasionally, though, Jimmie would not be sure. One day when a rather seedy and lonely-looking young man insisted upon entering, Jimmie's instincts told him to call Jack, who looked and said, "Tell this 'Lamont' man we're filled to capacity." Then Jack did a double take. . . . Lammot? . . . Du? . . . and quickly bowed and enthusiastically welcomed into the club the man, who stood quietly at the bar and drank. "Can you imagine," Jack scolded Jimmie, "*you* want to keep our young *Du Pont*, of the *Delaware Du Ponts*!"

Jimmie had been a dishwasher down the street at Leon & Eddie's before he was hired to take over walloping the pots at "21." One day Jack and Charlie were whispering in Yiddish back in the kitchen, the place where they discussed private matters, and Jimmie, standing nearby, chimed in. Startled at finding not a freckle-faced Irishman as they had thought him to be but a nice Jewish boy washing dishes, Jack and Charlie trusted Jimmie immediately—he was one of them—and they propelled him to the front door as receptionist to replace Mac. Since he was quick to memorize the club's roster of famous names and faces, the customers loved him. In fact, Jimmie did have a fine facility for segregating "the Brooks Brothers shirts from the Sanforized models." He once said, "The day I can't distinguish, I quit." He retired from the club in 1955 at the age of sixty-six, when he could no longer remember names, and it is rumored that he died a millionaire.

In addition to cliques of stars, writers, and the social set, there was also a large sporting and horsey crowd, and many asked Jimmie to take bets on the horses. Unfortunately, he would often forget to call in the bets. One day a thousand-dollar bet was taken and it slipped his mind. Finding the money in his pocket later that night, Jimmie hastily called the bookie to find that the horse had come in last anyway. "Well," Jimmie said philosophically, "no one ever bets on a winner."

Another unexpected dividend of Jimmie's was, as Bob Cooke told the story, from Myron Selznick, who was in "21" for dinner and on his way out had asked Jimmie if he could change a thousand-dollar bill.

"I've only got a hundred and thirty-eight dollars. You're welcome to it," said Jimmie helpfully. Selznick took it and handed the thousand-dollar bill to Jimmie. "Hold it for me until tomorrow," said Selznick. When he returned for lunch the next day, Jimmie proffered him the thousand-dollar bill. "Keep it," said Selznick.

Jimmie's tips were so heavy that he was known to make daily trips back and forth to the bank with his folding money; he kept his silver in polished wooden boxes, each 36 by 6 by 6 inches and fitted out for specific coins. A tip in those days was anywhere from a quarter to five bucks, and since everyone tipped right and left and coming and going, Jimmie did well. Well enough, that is, for Jack and Charlie to call a halt, deciding that the tips belonged to them. Jimmie resigned, leaving such chaos at the front door that Charlie had to go looking for him and hired him back.

Another legendary (and wealthy) staffer was "Red" Warner the doorman, who not only shuffled the Pierce-Arrows, Packards, Cadillacs, Rolls-Royces, and Brewsters that

Barmen Fisher and Lux, left and right, with Chef Henri Geib

fought for curb space outside the club but moonlighted for other speaks on Fifty-second Street as well. Red's tips were so good that he allegedly made enough money to buy a townhouse for himself across the street, where he kept his girl friend on one floor and rented out the rest, two floors going to speak-easies.

Such entrepreneuring activities of Red's (who today lives in the Bronx in one of the houses he supposedly owns there, and twice a year drops into "21" to pay his respects) provoked many a conversation in "21," and one day a lively argument commenced about just how many speaks there really were on the block. Barroom friend Robert Benchley and Jack set off to do a little social research, visiting and drinking down to Sixth, where the rumbling El turned them eastward to the south side of the street. They finally reached the mansion of William Henry Vanderbilt,

heir of "robber baron" Commodore Cornelius Vanderbilt of steamship and railroad fame; by then neither could remember why they had set out in the first place, but they rang that last bell anyway, only to be turned away by a very indignant butler. Their research might have been lost forever had not Benchley ticked off the speaks they went in and out of in a little notebook which he found later in his pocket, when he was functioning again: a whooping thirty-eight speaks on one block. Having rung a few other private bells besides Vanderbilt's on their journey along the street, they provoked one dowager to put up a sign on her door reading "This is *not* an illicit resort." So many pranksters scratched out the "not" that the woman finally changed her sign to "This is a *private* residence. Do not ring."

Fifty-second Street between Fifth and Sixth Avenues was indisputably the wettest

"21's" back-room-bar people shooting their biological systems

strip in New York. Speakeasies freely poured out booze and hot Dixieland jazz by the avant garde of white and black musicians, the latter who came in the twenties to be recognized beyond Harlem and receive the acclaim their talents were rightfully due. While they came downtown bringing "soul music," downtowners went uptown to Harlem, to Smalls' Paradise, Connie's Inn, and the Cotton Club, owned by bootlegger Owney Maden and bootleg king Arnold Rothstein, a club where, ironically, no blacks were allowed. As Pete Kriendler remembers today, "During Prohibition and even through the forties, Harlem was the place we went not only to hear music but to eat 'yardbird' [fried chicken], 'strings' [spaghetti], and black-eyed peas and spareribs with collards."

Until the mid-twenties, Fifty-second Street had been like others in the neighbor-

hood, a quiet residential thoroughfare lined with Victorian brownstone townhouses owned by wealthy families with such names as Potter, Rhinelander, and Baruch. When the City Board of Estimates rezoned the area in 1926 to allow commercial rentals, the exodus began, leaving a radically changed populace. Families took to the suburbs, riding the Rolls and rails to Westchester, Con-

necticut, and Long Island. The area became a collection of speaks and love nests as mobsters, gigolos, kept women, and businessmen staked out their claims against the anticipated appearance of Radio City. Jack & Charlie's was king of the block, but it had notable speakeasy neighbors including Tony Soma's "Tony's," a place frequented by magazine people and considered second in popularity to "21." Also there were the Club 18, the Yacht Club, Pop Reilly's Tavern, and Leon & Eddie's with their famous sign: "Through these portals the most beautiful girls in the world pass out."

Fifty-second Street joints were often raided, but it was said that Jack & Charlie's wasn't bothered because the big iron gate made the Prohibition agents mistake it for a police station and besides, they couldn't afford either the liquor or the food.

No one in the New York restaurant business has ever been able to hold a candle to Jack Kriendler for sheer personality, or for receiving so much newspaper space, including page-one coverage. There have been others equally or more loquacious, opinionated, and tyrannical, but none as calculatedly and obviously eccentric. Healthy extrovert Jack traveled about town dressed in full cowboy attire, complete with holster and guns and fringed shirt, frontier pants, fancy Western boots, and a Stetson. Riding in a Ford convertible dressed in these clothes, he would make "wet" deliveries to pet patrons during Prohibition, stopping at houses on Park and Fifth Avenues and those tiny black-and-white townhouses that lined the eastern side of Sutton Place. Jack had a habit of overtipping doormen and service people with silver dollars, one of his personal trademarks, leaving a trail behind him that even a blind cop could have followed. Since many patrons wanted home supplies of liquor, enterprising Jack and Charlie figured that there was no reason to leave friends to the mercy of boot-

leggers, especially when the club could make the sales and realize the profits.

Louis Sobol once described Jack in the New York *Journal-American* as "Two-Trigger Jack," a nickname that stuck for life. It grew out of Jack's love of horses and the Old West, where he liked to spend his vacations. He was, as Sobol said, "a man who, in chaps and ornate cowboy shirts, dusting his $10,000 silver saddle with an imported monogrammed handkerchief, will stand at a bar, preferably in Palm Springs or Tucson or Phoenix, tossing off drink after drink with you, leading the choral assembly in cowboy or nostalgic chants, riding his trusty mustang hard and true and relentlessly with no sign of fatigue." According to columnist Bill Corum, Jack rode with spurs that jingle-jangled, and in New York he often would mount up on the big saddle he kept in the lobby of "21," just to prove that he really could ride. As Corum joked, "Of course, he belonged no farther west than the Manhattan Transfer. But he knew it and the nice part was that he could laugh with it, too." Undeterred by public jesting, Jack was known to give away gifts of cowboy clothes and jewelry—belt buckles, spurs, hats, and scarf pins set with diamonds, rubies, and sapphires.

Charlie loved horses too, but more quietly—even shyly. As indoor sportsman Bill Hardey remembers, "Charlie rode that thing —his horse—until the day he died." Both Jack and Charlie had their riding habits made by Rodeo Ben (*né* Lichtenstein), a fashioner of riding clothes and the owner of a firm that has operated out of Philadelphia since 1928. As Rodeo Ben says, "I met Jack at a Madison Square Garden rodeo, and when he found out my business he took me home to '21', where I measured them up some clothes and became their Western tailor. At the time, Jack was on his way to Palm Springs and he took a whole Pennsylvania Railroad car to himself for the trip. Five Western musicians sent Jack off from the

New York station in a style to which he was accustomed—living like a king." Twelve cases of champagne and liquor were stashed in his cross-country home, causing Charlie, who was seeing Jack off, to stand mopping his brow and delving into one pocket after another where, W. C. Fields–style, he always kept different-shaped flasks, one for each kind of liquor. Charlie wore conservative, classic riding clothes, but Jack's passion was for the flamboyant and magnificent. His wardrobe for his favorite game—cowboying—boasted 130 shirts, 160 pairs of pants, 36 ten-gallon hats, 3 silver saddles, 26 pairs of boots, 24 belts, 20 complete rodeo suits, and, as the story goes, quite a few dozen odds and ends of cowboys accoutrements; no one ever counted such things as guns, spurs, and neckerchiefs.

Jack's back-up nickname was "The Baron," which perfectly fitted his baroque, Viennese personality and his cutaways, sable-lined overcoat, and shirts of soft silk. His "city" wardrobe provoked Mark Hellinger to poke fun at Jack and Charlie and their passion for clothing by writing in the early thirties that in the Village days, "Charlie was a plump youth with plenty of hair on his head and very little on his face. Jack was a wide-eyed lad with one suit that always fitted him perfectly. It all goes to show what success will do to people. Today, Charlie goes around with no hair on his head and plenty on his face, and Jack has 420 suits—not one of which fits him at all."

It was whispered that Jack enhanced his formidably military carriage by wearing a tight girdle, which explains, some intimates say, why he rarely bent over. Be that as it may, he had an undeniably grave, haughty, and majestic air, with his head held high and back ramrod straight. A close friend recalls how Jack constantly worked at improving his elocution, and how he used to make the friend accompany him down to the club cel-

lar to hear Jack practice an upper-class accent. Jack paced about the club with eyes gleaming like locomotive headlights, deigning to smile bleakly only when something was so obviously humorous that only a stiff would stare. A major ceremony occurred each day when Jack went into the kitchen to taste the sauces. The staff stood with bated breath until the master nodded confirmation, then broke into smiles of relief. Or sometimes silent giggles, such as when Jack would go into the little open phone booth in the lobby and, with a three-piece band to back him up, loudly—and off-key—whack away at a love song beamed to actress Arline Judge in Hollywood. When he finished, and to cover his antic, he would put out the light in the booth and turn and berate little Raymond, the lobby attendant, for having left it on and wasting electricity; then he would bend down and pick up a twenty-dollar bill from the floor, telling Raymond that if he'd been more alert he would have seen the bill first. Of course, Jack was dropping the money himself.

Charlie's financial management of the business was less dramatic than Jack's opera-

tion, but it had color of its own. During the first year of the operation on Fifty-second Street, three unwelcome visitors appeared one day and tried to barge into the club. They were representatives of Jack ("Legs") Diamond, a kingpin of the underworld and a bootlegger, hijacker, kidnapper, extortioner, and dope dealer. Of all the gangsters in town, he had the reputation of being the most sadistic, his favorite form of entertainment being to burn the bare soles of his captive's feet. As the killer of dozens of gangsters —by his own hand or by contracts he let out —Legs had been shot up so often that he was known as "The Clay Pigeon." He was a silent partner of many speaks, as well as a "take" artist of the first water. He is thought to have caused the disappearance of ten innocent employees and bystanders at the Hotsy Totsy Club on Fifty-second Street to prevent their testifying to a murder in which Legs was involved.

Legs now wanted part of the "21" operation—the biggest plum in town. When Charlie was presented with this demand, he turned sheet white—as he always did when he got mad—and in spite of the consequences, he took a swing. Jimmie joined him, and the brawl began, with the two men dusting the hoodlums in a way reminiscent of the Red Head days and throwing them out into the street. Legs sent word that he was putting contracts out on Jimmie and Charlie, but as luck would have it, before they found themselves on the other end of a gun or a match, Legs himself was wiped out. Charlie later said, "This reminded me of our Village Days. I guess the old adrenalin just got up and my reaction was automatic."

Left page, Mr. and Mrs. Damon Runyon and actor George Raft being bussed by Arline Judge. This page, Heywood Broun, Pied Piper of Jack and Charlie's Drinking Set.

5

"21" Slaps
the Hands of
Uncle Sam

After a short while into the Depression, many restaurants, hotel dining rooms, and speakeasy clubs about town were so desperate for business that they not only hired press agents—who came into their own during this period—to feed the Broadway columnists choice tidbits about their establishments, but they all but dragged columnists in off the streets in hope of a freebie plug. But "21" viewed them with a wary eye—who needed to take the chance of having an illicit business blurbed in the papers?—and with the exception of two old friends, Mark Hellinger and Heywood Broun, they permitted no columnists on the premises. But that didn't stop the loud-voiced Walter Winchell, who, though he'd never set foot through the door of Jack and Charlie's house, let the world know about it by running in his *Daily Mirror* column in 1930 a piece headed "A Place Never Raided, Jack & Charlie's at 21 West

Fifty-second Street." While this could have been innocent reporting from the famous W.W., it did not turn out harmless. The inevitable happened: Shortly after Winchell's column came out, "21" was raided. The raid made front-page news and also gained for Jack and Charlie the name of "Kings of Imported Liquor." It was an interesting case in terms of Prohibition law, and as attorney Julius Hallheimer says, "That was *some* case . . . *some* case. And if the prosecution had been successful, it would have been the finish of '21.'"

"The raid," as Hallheimer recalls, "was made not by local Revenue agents, who were friendly to '21,' but by Federal agents from Washington under the direction of a man by the name of John Calhoun, who claimed he made the raid under the orders of Frederick Lohman, Assistant Secretary of the Treasury in charge of the administration of the Prohibition Act." The raid resulted in the arrest of ten men, Jack and Charlie, Mac, Bill Hardey, Frank Applegate Buchanan, and five employees. They were arrested and charged with conspiracy to import and traffic in liquor and spirits, and a misdemeanor in maintaining premises to sell liquor. Bond was fixed at one hundred thousand dollars.

A truly huge quantity of liquor had been taken from the house, which was ransacked by agents who went to the private upstairs rooms and broke open bureau drawers and trunks, took away coin and stamp collections that were not contraband, as well as business records of the club. They also took cans of ether, two hypodermic syringes, and some medication.

The affidavit on which the search warrant was based asked the court to grant a warrant to search the entire premises on the basis that the whole building was used as a nightclub. It also contained statements that there were hostesses there and that dancing took place on the upper floors. Says Hallheimer, "These were untruthful statements. I immediately recognized that since there were ten men involved, I would have to have assistance in leading the defense. I asked Charles Dickerman Williams, a lawyer friend who was formerly a secretary to Justice Taft of the United States Supreme Court, and Kenneth Simpson, a former Assistant U.S. Attorney, to be my associates. We immediately moved to set aside the search warrant on the ground that the affidavit on which it was based was false, untruthful, and irregular.

"I contended," Hallheimer continued, "that since the affidavit was false, there should be applied here a legal maxim, *'Falsus in uno es falsus omnibus'* (False in part is false in all). Interestingly, the news media got hold of this, and there were statements in the press of government agents being charged with robbery, burglary, and ransacking the house and upstairs bedrooms. This

brought Mr. Lohman up from Washington, and now the government was on the defensive. What we were particularly interested in was getting back those books. The government came into Court and contended, when this came up for a hearing before Judge William Bondy, that the books and records were not seized from upstairs, but were found in the telephone booth of the restaurant . . . a silly claim.

"We had a great number of conferences with the U.S. Attorney, and finally his representatives agreed to drop the conspiracy charge and all the charges in the case, and would be satisfied with a plea of guilty from Jack and Charlie to 'possession of liquor,' a minor, innocuous accusation. Before Judge Francis J. Coleman, the judge I picked, the entire case was thrown out against the other eight men, the conspiracy charge thrown out, and all seized property was directed to be returned; Jack and Charlie pleaded 'possession,' and they received a fine of fifty dollars each, and they were later pardoned. This was the result of this big case involving one hundred thousand dollars' bail, in those days a lot of money, which ended in a terrible defeat for the U.S. government, and proves that you *can* slap the hands of Uncle Sam.

"Many people were interested in the ether, syringes, and medication aspect of this case, which we simply explained: Ether was used by the waiters to clean grease spots off their uniforms; medication and syringes were the possession of Charlie's cousin, Dr. William Bernfeld, connected with the Veterans Administration, who had been in the club the afternoon of the raid and left these items there when he changed his clothes."

Julius Hallheimer recalls an article that he and John T. de Graff collaborated on for *Century* magazine, in 1928, called "Why Conspiracy," and subtitled "Conviction Possible without an Illegal Act Committed." It gives a good insight into conspiracy and the ridiculous circumstances that existed as the charge was applied to Prohibition. It seems that back then an Indiana jury attained nationwide prominence by acquitting four men charged with "Conspiracy to Violate the National Prohibition Act." As the article relates, "The defendants were officers and salesmen of companies engaged in manufacturing and shipping unfermented grape juice. The juice shipped in sealed barrels constituted no violation of law. But when the purchaser ex- posed the juice to the air for thirty days, nature's knavery accomplished the rest by transforming it into an insidious beverage known as wine. . . . A number of editors were deeply mystified over the nature of the crime committed. The Norfolk *Virginia-Pilot* remarked, 'It would be carrying Prohibition to extraordinary lengths to affirm that while one may purchase virgin grape juice he is to be held responsible for any loss of chastity that the juice may suffer by reason of its being

Hap Flanigan, left, and Jack agree with Julius Hallheimer's "The more laws made, the more avenues open to graft"

left to its own devices.' [This law] viewed retrospectively . . . does not differ from the law of England in the Middle Ages, when a clergyman was convicted of treason for certain objectionable passages contained in a sermon found in his study, despite the fact that the sermon had never been preached or published."

This article further explains the conspiracy law by noting that if a friend calls up a bootlegger and asks for whisky, "an overt act is committed which makes you both guilty of conspiracy and subject to a long prison term if convicted. Whereas, if you had taken the whisky with you and completed the offense, the punishment for the crime itself would be the imposition of a nominal fine. . . . A person can be tried both for conspiracy to commit the offense and committing the offense as well. . . . The crime of illegally transporting liquor is only a misdemeanor; but on the identical facts you can be indicted for 'conspiracy to transport liquor,' and on similar proof can be convicted of a felony. . . . Thus the statute converts a misdemeanor into a felony."

Under the Volstead Act, any violation of its provisions was considered a misdemeanor; the Mullan-Gage Law, a New York State law set up in 1921 to enforce Prohibition, said that the possession or sale of intoxicating liquor as a first offense was a misdemeanor. But the second offense and every subsequent one was a felony. According to the Baumes Laws of New York, enacted in 1926, "any person who has been three times convicted of a felony shall, upon conviction of a fourth and subsequent felony, be sentenced to life imprisonment." You *did* have to be brave to run a speakeasy!

Hallheimer, attorney for "21" until 1966,

recalling the peculiar days of Prohibition, says: "I was a pretty busy man then. . . . We knew how to operate in those days, we each had our own territories. A Mr. Cashin had all the restaurants and speakeasies from Westchester up to Albany, a Mr. Halley had all the rum-runners for bringing liquor into New York, and I had the New York restaurants and speaks. On New Year's Eve, I always stayed home because I used to get fifteen to twenty calls from 11:00 p.m. on from my clients who had violated Prohibition laws. I would meet my people down at the house of the U.S. Commissioner of the Fifth Abeyance on West Tenth Street, with whom I would set bail. . . . Ironically, when we got to the commissioner's house we found *him* drunk!

"That was a most unusual era, we'll never have anything like it again. Prohibition was observed in the breach rather than in the acceptance. There used to be an Ipana toothpaste ad in magazines concerning pyorrhea, saying that four out of five will get it. With respect to liquor, we used to say that four out of five will get it, and the fifth knows *where* to get it."

Left page, Jack's funhouse and gardens in bucolic Hampton Bays. Right, all the comforts of home plus a "Wall Street reporter"

In 1931, Jack and Charlie, with money to burn in their pockets, took to the country—excited as city kids who had never seen a cow—to invest in land near Hampton Bays, Long Island. Charlie bought twenty acres of land up on a bluff and stocked it with livestock, turkeys, and ducks. Jack bought some land with a small house, adding extensions for guest quarters and a large patio with a tremendous barbecue pit and roasting oven. In the basement of the house he designed a replica of the "21" barroom, installing the original bar from the Puncheon Grotto on Forty-ninth Street, which Jack had stored away at the time of their speakeasy move hoping to use it one day in his own private barroom. On the back of the property he built a gatekeeper's cottage.

At first Jack and Charlie planned to use the properties as weekend retreats where they could get away from the speakeasy—a land where the sun never shone and electricity was a way of life. They also intended to become gentleman farmers, supplying meat, fowl, and produce for the club. Though the intent was good, the business side of the venture never got off the ground. Jack's house quickly turned into the scene for a series of endless weekend parties, invitations to which summoned the devout from "5:30 until Tuesday," as the drinking saying used to go. Bill Hardey handled the bar, Charlie and Hallheimer circulated among the guests, and Jack did the cooking—with an astonishing zest and ability—complete in full cowboy regalia. There was always a big party on Saturday night when a trencherman's meal was served, the antithesis of dinner at the gourmet club. Slated to begin about 6:30 p.m. on the patio under Japanese lanterns and to end about midnight, Jack's culinary performance was preceded by Bill's Block Busters, special, double-sized mint juleps with cognac floated on the top. "Those supercharged juleps never failed to shatter the ego of even the most robust drinkers," Hallheimer recalls. "After the second or third, one generally 'capitulated' unconditionally. Bill served them freely, and gleefully waited for the unexpected to happen—and it did."

Jack and Hallheimer booze at the Bays bar while friends, at right, lunch country-style

The evening of eating would take twenty-five to seventy-five people through marvelous wines and a first course of caviar, Gardiner's Island oysters by the dozens or pecks of steamers, followed by lobsters from Montauk. Steaks or a big haunch of beef or a whole baby lamb, cooked crispy outside and juicy inside, would make up the entrée, which was served with roasted potatoes, a sizable quantity of freshly picked Country-Gentleman corn, fresh salads of leafy lettuce with an oil and lemon juice dressing and succulent bursting-ripe tomatoes with fresh tarragon, basil, or dill—everything from the kitchen garden, including spinach creamed à la Jack, a dish known to many because it has been on the "21" menu for years now.

Instead of being out on the town enforcing the Mullan-Gage Law, the Hampton Bays police force, as well as half of the Suffolk County force, visited at Jack's house late on Saturday nights to enjoy his fine "brands" of hospitality. Considering the facts that Hampton Bays was a port that the rum-runners were known to put into at night, that the gatekeeper's cottage on the Kriendler property never housed guests or a gatekeeper, and that Jack and Charlie drove into town

The very, very British style of golf and mode of dress, 1931

each Monday morning in heavily loaded cars, it was not difficult for friends to put two and one together and come up with another reason why Jack and Charlie had become country gentlemen.

Regardless of the hour the party broke up on Saturday night, Jack arose—at a time un-sober for his guests—to lope along the beach, then hustle back to the home range to start Sunday lunch. In practice for later appearances on the "21" menu, he concocted such dishes as ratatouille, patchwork-colored with onions, beans, zucchini, eggplant, peppers, tomatoes, and herbs; and bouillabaisse, done up from local seafood, arriving *at table* in full steam, earth-orange of saffron, and ready to accept forks and crusty bread into its fragrant midst. Or there was crisp-skinned Long Island duckling, one for each person to disjoint and eat with the hands while quaffing Burgundy. Both led the way to strawberries, which were sweet, small, and dense-textured, as berries knew how to grow back in that era, and a crown of real, unadulterated, tart-sweet, spoonable heavy cream.

In the true Continental fashion of a stylish and exclusive city club having a counterpart retreat in the country, later that same year, 1931, Jack and Charlie took over the lease of the Westchester Embassy Club in the picturesque and lush hills of North Castle on Route 22 between Armonk and Bedford Village, New York. This genteel establishment, geared to fight the perverse act of Prohibition outside the city limits, offered to the country carriage trade such magnificent facilities as a sumptuous resort hotel, terraces for sipping and dancing under the moonlight, a sand-beached swimming pool, a stable of saddle horses with a show and jumping ring, and the very latest in sports facilities: tennis courts and a splendid eighteen-hole golf course. Lawn tennis had come a long way during the twenties, and golf had also come into vogue, and across America

anyone of any status and social scale carried tennis rackets and golf clubs and played "chase the little white ball." In fact, golf courses were being built throughout the land as determinedly as ants build hills. Predictably, Jack and Charlie, resplendent in white knickers, V-necked cashmere sweaters, and striped ties, pursued both games as avidly as their privileged clientele, which included the Roosevelts, the Farleys, and the Whitneys. The boys rode and drank with judges, district attorneys, and attorney generals, who frequented not only the Embassy Club but also "21"—not contacts to sneeze at should one have legal troubles.

Under a board of distinguished governors, which included Dan Topping, Herbert Gerlach, Julius Hallheimer, Frederick Holbrook, and Francis T. Hunter, the exclusive club established a pre-eminent position as the most elite country-club resort in America. Membership dues were two hundred dollars a year, and members could come on weekdays and weekends to participate in sports, stroll the grounds like prancing peacocks, watch horse shows, and play the slot machines and roulette—that is, when the club manager did not have the wheel hidden under the hay in the stable, since gambling was about as legal as whisky, which was moved back and forth from town to country mostly in Jack's big black Cadillac.

Johnny Seeman remembers one day when he drove Jack to Westchester and came back with a supply of Bristol Cream sherry. Clipping along the Bronx River Parkway, Johnny turned on the radio and heard that Federal Revenue agents were stopping traffic in a roadblock up ahead. He pulled over on the shoulder, got out, and hid the bottles in the loose stones in a wall by the Kensico Dam. To this day, Johnny can't remember exactly

Top: Two "21" regulars: Bill Hardey and Julius Hallheimer. Bottom, newlyweds Charlie and Molly Berns. Right, friends in the country

where he put it, though he's beavered a lot of loose stones up there by that dam ever since.

When not commuting back and forth between Westchester, Long Island, and Manhattan, Jack and Charlie, dedicated businessmen with iron discipline but also two guys who knew how to play when it was time to play, started traveling and seeing the world. They went to their favorite Palm Springs, to Europe—where they recruited personnel for the club—and to Cuba. In 1931, after Charlie had taken a three-week cruise to the island and come back with glowing stories of "Habana," cha-cha-cha, black bean soup, *culantro*, rum, and daiquiris *real*, Jack started off on the same trip. But this one ended in tragedy. To outdo Charlie, Jack made the trip by private yacht from Florida, borrowing boat and crew from a Wall Street friend. Jack's cousin Dr. Bernfeld accompanied him on the trip. On their way home, driving through Florida, Jack went off the road in a rain storm and the doctor hit the windshield and was killed. Jack survived the crash but with a badly ripped leg.

Recuperating in New York, Jack occupied himself with a side venture, which was to help cover Bill Hardey in opening Bill's Gay Nineties on East Fifty-fourth Street, in the property the boys had purchased prior to moving to Fifty-second. Putting about seven thousand dollars into the operation for equipment and all supplies, Jack finished off the décor by setting four hundred silver dollars into the floor. Bill's spot became famous overnight, and for years when people leaving "21" asked for a place to spend the rest of the evening, Bill's Gay Nineties would be the suggested club. Jack and Charlie eventually pulled out their interest, and Henry Tannenbaum went into partnership with Hardey for a period of about twenty-five years, after which Tannenbaum pulled out and Hardey had his club to himself until he retired in the sixties.

6

Bottle, Bottle, Who's Got the Bottle?

The last Prohibition raid of "21" occurred in June 1932. It was just after noon when Jimmie, at the door, confided to Jack, "I feel apprehensive hunches in the presence of cops and robbers." Giving Charlie the high sign, Jack hurried to the barroom, where he tinkled two glasses together and said, "Ladies and gentlemen, please finish your drinks and keep calm, we might have a few visitors." Jack signaled to Gus at the bar, who, with the help of the waiters, racked all glasses and bottles on the bar shelves. A buzzer sounded, and to the amazement of everyone, they saw the shelves behind the bar tip over backward toward the wall, and their dozens of liquor bottles suddenly vanish, leaving only empty shelves, which returned to their normal position. There had been not a sound except for the distant harmonies of crashing glassware, followed by a heady bouquet. The headwaiter, dressed in the formal attire of his profession, said, "In other words, bottoms up, it's a raid," and he asked for and received permission to slip into a chair and join a conveniently formal dinner party. Self-preservation: the first law of nature.

Jimmie's Runyonesque suspicion that there might be agents on the street had been sound. While Jack had tended to the downstairs, Charlie had made a quick phone call to a friendly Prohibition agent. Visitors were indeed nearby.

Eight Revenue men appeared at the door and presented a search warrant, telling Jimmie that unless he opened up they planned to break the door down. As the threatened lunge began, the door opened and into the welcoming lobby tumbled the Feds. Chagrined but inside, the whuffing raiders started their work.

For several hours the men crawled over the house, measuring closets, the depth of staircases, ceilings, doors, floors, using probes through plaster, pushing and poking at furniture, and shoving their hands down into the chef's sauce pots. They found nothing. By late afternoon they had called in two more men, who carefully tapped and sluiced their measuring tapes in and out of little leather cases, arguing and making calculations. One man went up on the roof and, thinking that he had found where the evidence was buried, had himself lowered down into the water tank on a rope. But he suddenly remembered that he couldn't swim, and another man had to go down.

This ten-man team of Prohibition agents was in the building nearly twelve hours. The closest they came to finding anything was in the cellar, where the smell of wine and liquor was unmistakable. An agent borrowed a claw hammer from a porter and tapped the cellar walls, striking an area with the hammerhead and then placing the wooden handle to his ear. Speculative evidence based on odor was not enough for an arrest. "Proof" had to be somewhere, but the agents could not find a drop of beer, whisky, or wine. At last, with tails between their legs, knowing they had been made into a crew of suckers, the raiders left. As they got into their cars, each had a parking ticket: Charlie had been on the phone again.

Five minutes later, Charlie, Mac, and Jack were laughing and toasting one another with snifters of brandy, and the bar shelves were once again sparkling bright with bottles. Customers had drifted through the front door and ordered drinks, and Chef Henri had resumed preparation of supper dishes, sprinkling sherry into green turtle soup, cognac into the Faisan à la Périgourdine, Grand Marnier into sauce for the *crêpes* Suzette Paradise, and a little Westphalian ham and *verre de vin* for himself.

More than forty thousand dollars' worth of wine alone was stashed within a few feet of the raiders when they searched the cellars, and many hundreds of cases of wines and liquors were elsewhere in the club. Jack and Charlie had a secret, and what a secret. After surviving the big raid of 1930, the boys knew they had to go completely secret in their operation so that not even a teaspoonful of evidence could be found against them. Conferring with "21" designer Frank Applegate Buchanan and builder Sol Lustbader, they plotted, planned, and built the most sophisticated secret electrical hideaway system of any speak in town. This is the way the upper floors of the house operated:

Between the outermost iron-grille door with the square peep hole and the inner set of doors with curtains was a vestibule fitted with four push buttons, all in different places and all concealed. Jimmie could always reach one of them, no matter what position he might be wrestled into by rough Revenue men trying to break through. All the buttons were connected to a signal system inside the house which set off a warning bell, alerting the barman to a raid.

The club could count on a good three to four minutes of leeway time between the doorman's pushing the button and any forced entry—time for waiters to swoop up the evidence and have it disappear from the bar shelves. But where did the bottles and glasses go? Shades of Orson Welles, Vienna, and *The Third Man*—if one had looked down the opening revealed behind the back bar as the shelves tipped over, one would have seen a brick-lined chute with iron spikes jutting from the walls, arranged so that bottles would strike the spikes and shatter, and then fall on down to an iron grating to smash completely any stubborn glass. Under the grating was an opening leading down past the basement drain and into the New York sewerage system, into which

Charlie on the lookout for "Feds" who might be sneaking up to the speakeasy door

64

everything ran off to disappear forever!

Moving upstairs in the club, one found— or better, didn't find—a series of secret closets. The first was reached by entering a closet in which a few waiters' coats, neckties, and collars hung on hooks. Innocent enough, until an ordinary table knife was held horizontally between two coat hooks so that it touched both of them simultaneously. A buzzing would occur, and suddenly the back wall would swing away on hinges to reveal a very narrow room with shelves full of wine.

Two flights up, on the fourth floor, was another closet, again with a heavy secret door which was opened by thrusting one end of the coat-hanger pole deeply into its metal wall brace so that electrical contact was made inside the socket. This closet was bare, but it led into another secret room, opened only by taking a small piece of iron, two or three inches long, and running it slowly along a wall mounting. A buzzing sound accompanied the moving shelves, which opened to reveal a dungeon within a dungeon, its shelves heavy with wine and the closet temperature controlled to protect the cases of Montrâchet 1889, Romanée-Conti 1880, and fine vintages of Château Lafite-Rothschild. Jack and Charlie had not been in operation long enough to buy and hold their own wines, so their properly aged bottlings had been coming to them through special orders to European wine contacts and bootleggers, and also through the surreptitious purchase of wine cellars from estates around the East.

The last cache was also on the fourth floor but on the opposite side of the building. Here, another closet was wired so that one had to take a wire coat hanger and make contact between it and two brass coat hooks set into the closet wall. A wall would open to

Cavista Ralph Cerda, left, inserts key to cellar door. Right, stylish as the Twentieth-Century Limited: an early menu card from "21"

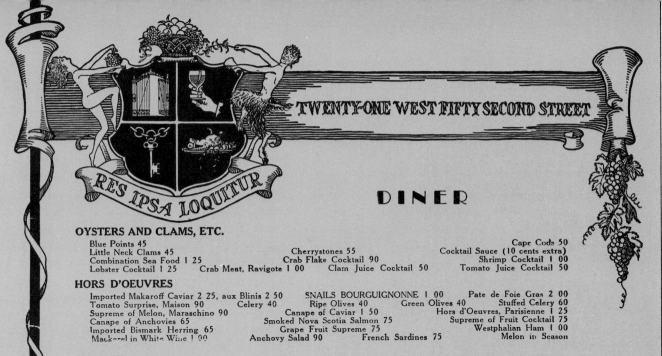

RES IPSA LOQUITUR

TWENTY-ONE WEST FIFTY SECOND STREET

DINER

OYSTERS AND CLAMS, ETC.
Blue Points 45
Little Neck Clams 45   Cherrystones 55   Cape Cods 50
Combination Sea Food 1 25   Crab Flake Cocktail 90   Cocktail Sauce (10 cents extra)
Lobster Cocktail 1 25   Crab Meat, Ravigote 1 00   Clam Juice Cocktail 50   Shrimp Cocktail 1 00
    Tomato Juice Cocktail 50

HORS D'OEUVRES
Imported Makaroff Caviar 2 25, aux Blinis 2 50   SNAILS BOURGUIGNONNE 1 00   Pate de Foie Gras 2 00
Tomato Surprise, Maison 90   Celery 40   Ripe Olives 40   Green Olives 40   Stuffed Celery 60
Supreme of Melon, Maraschino 90   Canape of Caviar 1 50   Hors d'Oeuvres, Parisienne 1 25
Canape of Anchovies 65   Smoked Nova Scotia Salmon 75   Supreme of Fruit Cocktail 75
Imported Bismark Herring 65   Grape Fruit Supreme 75   Westphalian Ham 1 00
Mackerel in White Wine 1 00   Anchovy Salad 90   French Sardines 75   Melon in Season

POTAGES
Cream of New Peas 45   Minestrone Italienne 45
Purée of Tomato 45   Consommé Vermicelli 40
Madrilène en Gelée 45   Onion Soup au Gratin 50
Petite Marmite Bouchère 55   Green Turtle au Sherry 65

POISSONS (Per Person)
Filet of English Sole, Bonne Femme 1 40
Broiled Pompano, Potato Chips 1 25
Baked Sea Trout, Russe 1 10
Fried Frogs' Legs, Tartar 1 25
Crab Flakes à l'Orientale 1 10
Soft Shell Crabs Sauté Provençale 1 25

ENTREES (Ready Per Person)
Roast Prime Ribs of Beef, Jardinière 1 70
(Half) Chicken Grain, Marengo 2 00
Steak de Veau Sauté, Egg Plant Orientale 1 30
Breast of Guinea Hen, Smitaine 1 90
Broiled Sweetbread, Virginia 1 60
Noisette of Lamb, Capucine 1 60
Mixed Grill, Gaufrette Potato 1 60

COLD DISHES
Sirloin of Beef Niçoise 1 65
Galantine of Capon, Parisienne 1 70
Viande Froide Assortis, Salade de Pommes de Terre 1 70
Carre d'Agneau, Broccoli Salad 1 65

LEGUMES
Purée of Celery 50
Succotash 60   Stewed Corn 50   New Beets au Beurre 45
Broccoli 75   Cauliflower 65   Lima Beans 50   Braised Celery 60
French Peas 50; Bonne Femme 65   String Beans 50   Carrots Vichy 50
Artichokes 65   Spinach 50   Creamed Spinach 60
New Corn Sauté 60   Brussels Sprouts 45   Oyster Bay Asparagus 90
Egg Plant, Orientale 60   Zucchini 50   Hearts of Palms, Mousseline 90

POMMES
Parisienne Persillées 40   Au Gratin 40   Anna 50   Lyonnaise 40   Sauté 40
Julienne 40   Hashed Brown 40; in Cream 50   Allumette 40
Candied Sweet, Louisanna 60

ENTREMETS GLACES
Berries in Season 50   Caramel Custard 50
Vanilla Ice Cream 50   Chocolate Ice Cream 50
Peach Melba 75   Pear, Belle Hélène 65
French Pastry 35   Fruit Tart 50   Petits Fours 40
Coupe St. Jacques 75   Coupe aux Marrons 75   Compote of Fruits 75
French Pancake 1 00   Apple Pancake 1 00
Cerises Jubilee 1 25   Baked Alaska (for 2) 2 00
Crepes Suzette, Paradise 1 50

CAFE-THES   Cafe Kirsch 1 25
Coffee with Cream 40   Demi-Tasse 25   Special Percolated Coffee 50
Orange Pekoe Tea 40   Kaffee Hag Demi-Tasse 30
Cafe Diable, Special 1 50

SALADS
Escarole	45
Martin	50
Mexicaine	60
Nicoise	60
Fresh Vegetable	1 00
Chiffonnade	50
Lettuce	40
Romaine	45
Mixed Green	50
Tomato and Lettuce	50
Alligator Pear	75
Roquefort or Russian Dressing, extra	25

FROMAGES
Cream Cheese	40
With Bar le Duc	65
Petit Gervais	35
With Bar le Duc	60
Camembert	45
English Stilton	60
Bel Paese	45
Imported Swiss	45
Gorgonzola	45
Cheddar	60
Port du Salut	45
Roquefort	50

Thursday, September 21, 1933

reveal a room some ten feet long and six feet wide jutting out over a stairway. If the agents had been more alert—they were tired when they got to this part of the house—they would have known by the depth of the staircase walls that some concealed space had to be there.

For further house security, a second button behind the bar short-circuited the elaborate electrical device that controlled access to these secret rooms. In such a case, even if the raiders had discovered the triggering devices, the locks wouldn't have worked for

wine. The club also needed a secret storage place that absolutely *no one* could penetrate.

And so the famous "21" wine cellar was built. That cellar of the club's Prohibition days, that cache of over two thousand cases of wine which a ten-man team of raiders could not find even though they stood alongside it, is the same cellar that is in the house today. Though most patrons have visited it at one time or another since Repeal, none has ever known the name of the man who designed the cellar and its famous secret door, nor the circumstances surrounding its con-

Cellar-door lock and strike plate

them. Dynamite alone would have got them inside the secret closets. During their first year of operation these hideaways offered adequate storage space, but the club had to expand its facilities as the wine and liquor inventories grew, as collections came in and space was needed for laying away young

struction. Now a condominium builder from Pompano Beach, Florida, Soll Roehner, tells here for the first time how he conceived and built the door and the famous wine cellar:

"Bill Liebowitz, a club regular, introduced me to Jack and Charlie as the only construction man who could build a secret warehouse within '21.' Bill assured the partners of my trustworthiness and special abilities, and I felt that they had placed their careers in my keeping when we shook hands on the deal. I was raised in the construction industry—gaining trade techniques from my father which had been handed down to him from his grandmother, who constructed loft buildings for sweat shops in New York during the last century. But my architectural and engineering studies never touched on secret-door and concealed-warehouse construction. This design was a great challenge;

and more sketches on scratch pads . . . no formal drawings to connect with my project were to fall into the wrong hands.

"It was necessary to construct a warehouse that could not be found by conventional measuring, and a concealed entrance was needed with a secret door of exquisite design and workmanship. I considered layouts and decided on building a brick door in the brick foundation wall connected to the easterly cellar. The door had to be of materials and construction similar to the adjacent wall so that tapping sounds would be consis-

Names famous during Prohibition: Golden Wedding, Echo Spring, and Tea Kettle

it required originality and resourcefulness, absolute secrecy was required, and I needed workmen whose loyalty and trust could be depended upon. Ben Crow, Ernie Roehner, my younger brother, and Joe Whitney were my principal artisans and close friends. I drew sketches on napkins at the restaurant

tent. Also, the door had to be strong enough to resist conventional tools if its secret location became known to pirates, enterprising hoods, or the law, and it had to be fitted precisely to circumvent someone's testing for air drafts with smoke from a cigarette. My computations indicated that such a door would

69

Anti-Prohibitionists converge on capitol

weigh more than two tons and would have to function with precision balance to avoid damage to the brick door as it met the brick jam stop. A concealed metal adjustment stop was fabricated so that the brick just kissed against brick as the door swung shut. In the locked position, the door had to be perfectly solid with no visible play. The lock had to operate without a conventional key, to be absolutely jam-proof, and to be lockable from the warehouse side in case of siege.

"I devised the lock and the strike plate, which has never failed. The strike plate has a roller device which was then unique, original, and essential to the precise closing. Every two or three years I inspect the big brick door and its lock, and it operates like the masterpiece it was intended to be.

"After building the '21' project, and though no one knew where it was of course, requests for secret doors and warehouses came to me through Jack and Charlie's friends. I always had to be concerned about secrecy, constantly searching for anyone who might be following me or my vehicles trying to locate my work. One day I realized that I had private knowledge of vast inventories of illicit liquor. No one customer asked questions regarding any one else's storage areas, but it was conceivable that kidnapping or torture could be brought to bear on me or my men. Also, the law was always trying to find a cache of contraband booze. I expressed my apprehensions to friends, who advised that I was the subject of a gentlemen's agreement among the mobs—and was designated to be harmless and protected.

"Many people over the years have tried to guess the secret opening device of the '21' wine cellar door. No one has been successful, but now, since so many employees and visitors to the cellar have learned how to activate the locking device, the management has sacrilegiously fastened a conventional iron hasp and padlock to my masterpiece. It is

difficult to be without fault, even for '21.' "

How does that door open? In the cellar the visitor is confronted with brick alcoves with no visible cracks. But take a piece of wire about eighteen inches long and insert it in a tiny hole—just the right one among millions of tiny holes in the bricks—thrust the wire all the way in, and a sharp, metallic click can be heard. Within seconds, with the application of minimal pressure, the white brick wall swings back, opening without a sound. Inside is a vast wine cellar of many rooms with bin after bin of bottles—a sight to make any wine-lover gasp. There is no

Campaigning Roosevelt gets a big cheer

other entrance or exit, and if the door mechanism should break, the entire building would have to be demolished to get into the cellar.

But when this raid occurred, who could suspect the collection's actual location? It was not in No. 21, but in the cellar of No. 19—the house next door. Jack and Charlie owned that house, ninety thousand dollars worth, registered in the name of Henry Tannenbaum. Little wonder the Federal agents were perplexed.

In the New York *World-Telegram* of July 26, 1932, author and critic George Jean Nathan delivered a marvelous satirical medal to Jack and Charlie in a discussion of the forthcoming presidential campaign: 'Jack and Charlie, of my favorite speakeasy, would make the best President and Vice President. And I am quite serious. The speakeasy makes money, and the customers and owners are happy. In what other business is that true? The speakeasy is the most efficiently run enterprise in America today. It is an independent unit except when the government horns in. Neither Mr. Hoover nor Mr. Mellon could run a speakeasy profitably and well. They have made a botch of much simpler things."

The revolt against Prohibition assumed serious proportions during the presidential campaign of 1932 when it became a national issue. The Democratic party was unequivocally for Repeal; the Republican plank was for a revival of the Eighteenth Amendment with some safeguards attached. The heat was on Washington and the slogan "Drink up" was applauded by such distinguished people as Bernard Baruch, Percy S. Straus, and Will Rogers.

In 1932, in Dizzy Dean's immortal words, Franklin D. Roosevelt "slud home." By December 1933, Prohibition was repealed by the passage of the Twenty-first Amendment which nullified the Volstead Act. The government had been made to look foolish and eat crow, and a wise President—whose speech writer, Sam Rosenman, hung out in "21"—knew that the whole bloody act of dryness had been nothing but ridiculous. The Great Foolishness was over. "Drink up," indeed.

Will Rogers, who said, "If you think the country ain't wet, just watch 'em drink"

7

Refreshing,
Isn't It?

"Hats were tossed high, and there was the greatest sight you'd ever seen in the club," Charlie once recounted. "We opened the iron gate and grille door wide, had huge deliveries of liquor stacked all over the place, from the lobby to the men's room. We sang corny songs and sat around on cases, used them as footrests, and swigged from bottle necks. . . . December 5, 1933, after thirteen years, ten months, eighteen days, eighteen hours, and fifty-five minutes, Repeal and free at last."

The dry debacle had been generous to the two kids who proved, as Pop Reilly once said, "that Prohibition was not only a bad law, but a violation of good taste." But, expectedly, Repeal for the club was a letdown, an anticlimax. The dining rooms stood desolate and quiet, action at the bar dwindled to its lowest ebb. Twenty-nine waiters and captains and eight chefs, a steward, two maids, four porters, and four barmen stood behind

some sixty empty chairs. Jack and Charlie conferred in the kitchen and asked, "With the clout and spice of the illegal gone, are we destined to survive only in memory as 'one of those funny places people used to go to?'"

Jack and Charlie almost went bankrupt that first year after Repeal. In town, the Depression still caused short money, and those who were spending demanded fresh thrills and new experiences. Hollywood stars and producers, Café Society, and the horsey and sporty sets who had frequented "21" spread out to soak up the novel pleasure of Perona's jungle of zebras called El Morocco, Sherman Billingsley's Stork Club, high on glossy boudoir satin and balloons, and Gene Cavallero's conservative Colony. They elevatored up to the Rainbow Room and strutted through Peacock Alley in the Waldorf-Astoria, captured the moods of The Versailles, House of Morgan, and Bea Lillie's

Montmartre.

Life at "21" had somehow lost its rosy cheeks. Almost unbelievably, the club let none of the staff go, and Jack and Charlie even met demands for higher wages as hotels and restaurants about town tried to pirate the "21" personnel. "We had ridden out Prohibition and offered ourselves as candidates for Leavenworth," Charlie later explained. "We condescended to give up the Westchester Embassy Club—just didn't renew the lease since Repeal had negated its noble purpose and it was a losing deal. But we couldn't give up '21.' And if we had let our people go, where and how would we have replaced

them if business turned? The lesson we learned was that in a crisis you make decisions and stick to them. We survived this period principally because we stuck to the record and the reputation we had built up—that was all we knew. Such regulars as Willard McKay, Ned Depinet, Herb Smith, and Chuck Luckman all stayed loyal to us, as did the Yale men."

Jack and Charlie, who grew up in a time of stress and emergency, displayed a combination of guts, character, and courage. Noth-

Beer is back in New York to help supply New York's "21," opulent booze-and-beer house for the very, very rich and famous

ing befitted their action more than the famous song of that era, Blind Boy Fuller's "Keep on Truckin'." And no one trucked more than Jack, whose personal life made "Mooey, Mooey Love" headlines and brought dubious publicity for the club. Jack was tall and handsome, a kind of Lothario, and his romances had always been the talk of the town. It was at this point, while romancing a married dame, that his escapades really made the news. The irate husband had his unfaithful wife's telephone tapped and transcriptions of the calls hit the papers. Jack was named as correspondent, and forever after that his friends made constant jokes about his gooey love affairs. Having Jack's love life sprayed across the papers did no harm at all to the club's business. Unattached young ladies practically hauled their beaux to "21," where they made come-on eyes at the romantic bachelor-proprietor. One invited him up to her home in Connecticut. On a warm summer day in 1934, Jack, in his big Cadillac convertible, with a wicker hamper loaded with champagne, *pâté*, caviar, *baguettes*, cold pheasant, pears, and Brie cheese, and a complete silver service with checkered tablecloth, was on his way to fetch his prospective lady love for a Rat and Mole's *Wind in the Willows* picnic. Whis-

tling an anticipatory tune, Jack—always a lousy and reckless driver—skidded around a corner on a dirt road near Greenwich. The car hit a tree, the picnic basket sailed out, and its contents scattered over the landscape. Then the tree fell over and smashed the hood of Jack's car!

Now that Repeal had made liquor trafficking legal once again, enterprising Jack and Charlie could see a big new profitable industry opening up. Anxious to be a part of any money action, and displaying their business acumen, early in 1934 they organized "21" Brands, Inc., a company designed to import and distribute the brands of wines, liquors, and liqueurs that they had been serving, and any other quality bottlings that might now begin to flow into the country and be produced once again in our own distilleries and wineries.

Ballantine's Scotch, the standard of the bar at "21," was one franchise the boys did not want to let slip through their fingers, so

steely-nerved Charlie put an ambitious plan into action, sending salesmen across the states to sell a commodity that they as yet had no right to distribute. Orders piled up, creating an influence on the Ballantine's representative that he could not easily ignore. After a handshake deal with Charlie, the boys had the exclusive Ballantine wholesale franchise rights in the United States. But then Jack and Charlie's plan for the team effort of importing, distributing, retailing, and consuming was nipped in the bud. State stat-

utes set up to govern the liquor industry precluded ownership of both a wholesale distributorship and a retail operation. Not only did the companies have to keep separate records, but the businesses could not be under one roof, or have connected doorways. As a result of this, the famous partnership of Jack and Charlie was dissolved, with Jack relinquishing his active interest in "21" Brands to Charlie and Charlie turning over his interest in the club and the real estate—houses No. 21 and 19—to Jack and Mac.

But how to separate fire and air? Impossible, especially when one hand fed the other. Charlie brought townhouse No. 17 adjacent to the club for eighty thousand dollars and gave his new "21" Brands headquarters a gay Continental air by decorating the windows and doors with colorful travel posters and pictures of foreign vineyards and towns. Every minute that he wasn't working in the Brands, he was padding about the club, lunching with Jack and Mac, and they all passed opinions on business together.

Charlie was a true marketing genius, and one of his beliefs was that California table wines would eventually come into their own. In the early part of the twentieth century this industry had been booming, but Prohibition laid the vineyards fallow, and it took some while for the vintners to get going again beyond their "sacramental" output. Charlie took on the white wines of Wente Brothers, the reds of Louis M. Martini, and champagne from Korbel, three of the finest vintners out of the West. He pioneered the selling of these brands, adding others over the years, and indoctrinated not only his employees but anyone else who came into the club. As Harry G. Serlis, president of the Wine Institute, says today, "The Kriendlers and their persuasive wine list, and Charlie Berns, were among the first of New York restaurateurs and distributors to recognize the

The three houses that Jack and Charlie built

unique quality of California wines." Charlie also paved the way for Tribuno vermouth, Bobadilla sherries, Hine cognac, Ezra Brooks bourbon, and a host of other fine wines and spirits.

Francis T. Hunter, a man famous in the shipping and newspaper business as well as on the tennis courts as a Davis Cup player, came in as president, and, with Charlie as chairman of the board, "21" Brands, Inc. moved into one of the most respected positions in the importing and distributing business. Soon the firm expanded into No. 23 West Fifty-second Street, acquiring the old Madison Lewis family mansion house in

1942 from the Young Women's Christian Association for ninety thousand dollars. In the early sixties, "21" Brands bought tiny No. 25, which was at that time adjacent to Leon & Eddie's nightclub.

In the lore of the New York liquor business, the penthouse of No. 23 became famous as a bachelor pad—and what a busy one it was—and for entertaining wholesalers; the parties there created a mystique that roughly paralleled brother "21" next door. Only a "litmus test" allowed the socially acceptable into the hallowed ground of the penthouse, where Francis Hunter's big-game trophies from Africa, India, and Alaska stood, sat, looked out, and supplied stools, sofas, rugs, and ash trays, à la the tropical safari trophy room. It was complete with a mahogany bar, and outside yawned a Mediterranean-tiled terrace with shrubbery so profuse that the birds gathered there and sang.

In 1970, "21" Brands, Inc. was sold to Foremost-McKesson, Inc., a move prompted by Charlie and Mac, who had himself gone over to the Brands in 1955 as treasurer. The sale took place just one year before Charlie's death in 1971 and shortly before Mac's death in 1973.

In the years of operation under its original ownership, several of the Kriendler and Berns clans joined the Brands, among them a Kriendler nephew, Kermit Axel, son of Augusta Kriendler Axelrod. He left the company in 1973 to become a consultant within the field and is now vice president of Knickerbocker Liquors Corp. Recalling the fastidiousness of his uncle Jack, and the character he set for "21," Axel reminisces: "What a martinet . . . one summer during college years, I worked as a food checker in the back of '21,' stationed by the service bar. I noticed that the bartenders got busy and somebody wanted a martini, so I decided to make one to help the waiter, since I was just standing there. As I was pouring it out, Uncle Jack came in and roared at me, 'You don't know enough to make drinks for *my* customers.' I started to defend myself, and that was the worst thing to do. All I said was 'Yes, sir.' A bartender to Jack was a very upper-strata employee, very important. In his opinion, no college kid like myself could make a good drink. No way. He really roasted me."

Not only was "21" Brands a colorful op-

eration, so were the salesmen in the early days. The staff was chiefly made up of out-of-work young playboys about town—on the loose at the end of the Depression—such as Esmond O'Brien and Eddie McIlvain, whose father was president of Bethlehem Steel, and struggling young David Niven, hired by Jack Kriendler, who, wary of a young Englishman like Niven, had him "fingerprinted at FBI headquarters," as the now-famous actor relates in his autobiography, *The Moon's a Balloon*. Niven also recalls that he was paid a forty-dollar-a-week retainer against ten per cent of the orders he brought in—which, it ought to be noted, tallied little. A story often

told on Niven relates how his favorite forms of "selling" were to sit in "21" with Barbara Hutton, or, when not with her, to meander down the street to Rose's Restaurant, there to deliver three bottles of Ballantine's and with the monies received stand at Rose's bar with friends and drink up the profits. Then he would go get another three bottles.

Far left, Kermit Axel with his Uncle Bob Kriendler. Near left, Francis T. Hunter in the trophy room of No. 23. Above, Jack

81

With Repeal, Fifty-second Street gained the name "Swing Street" because of the concentration of hot music by swing bands, belted out of the old speakeasies which had now turned to "clubs," the name Jack and Charlie also gave their place. But the difference between a club and a saloon, as Quentin Reynolds noted, "is that in a club you must keep your coat on at all times even in the summer and in a saloon you do not have to keep your coat on providing, of course, you are wearing a shirt. Then too a saloon is commonly called a 'workingman's club' and even when it is crowded at '21' you will very seldom find anyone present who works or who thinks of the word work with anything but mingled feelings of horror and disgust. . . . I will continue to call '21' a saloon or a barroom."

And crowded it was. By the mid-thirties, those who had strayed from "21" after Repeal slipped unobtrusively back, admitting

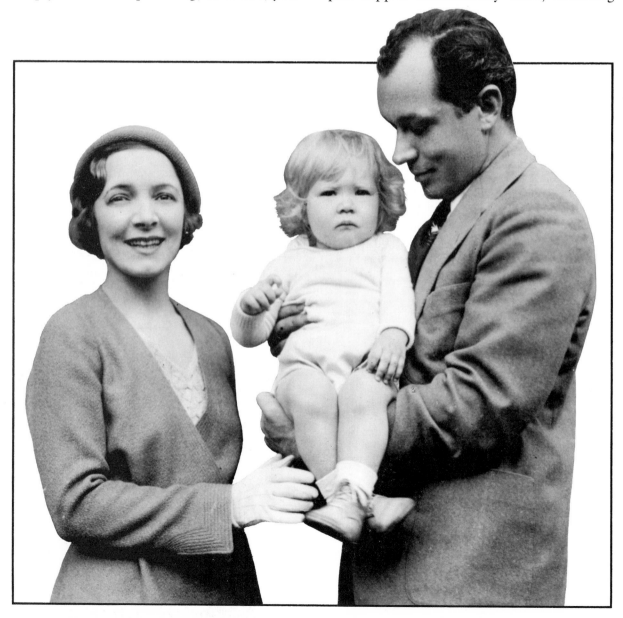

that they had found no other barroom like it in town. There was something about the place that folks had missed: its clubbiness, its clannishness, its coziness, the checkered cloths, Mac's singing, Jack's antics, neighbor Charlie's wry, warm smile, and the relaxed atmosphere where you were left alone to mingle freely, drink, dine, flirt, play pranks, and plan love affairs.

Jack & Charlie's was considered to be on a par with the Ritz Bar in Paris, the Savoy Grill in London, and Vienna's Bristol Hotel, popular hangouts that Americans had begun to discover as they continued the pattern of the twenties, sailing off to the Continent. The very rich, who are, as Fitzgerald noticed, different from the rest of us, flocked in to stand at the "21" bar and mix with the tweedy literati in an atmosphere thick with the contrast of money, humor, and bar jokes —some as old as last Tuesday, but all in innocent fun. If the twenties was a time of secret excess and life "underground," the mid-thirties had become an expansively open and social time. Thus was heralded the second great era in the life of "21," the open reign of Café Society.

Famous names and faces abounded in the "21" townhouse, the Westbury polo-playing crowd rubbing elbows with Groucho Marx (who addressed everyone he couldn't place as "Mr. Benson"), the quiet giant Bernard Baruch, who played off against that garrulous literary bar team of Ben Hecht and Charles MacArthur, a great Irishman who won the heart of his future wife, Helen Hayes, by thrusting at her a bag of peanuts with the remark, "I wish they were diamonds."

In the 1936 edition of the *Iron Gate of Jack & Charlie's "21,"* a tribute to the boys in which famous authors tried to outdo one another in contributing humorous articles

Left, Helen Hayes and Charles MacArthur with their daughter, and, at right, friend Ben Hecht

about their love affairs with the club, Charles MacArthur penned the following letter addressed to the Commissioner of Police, New York City:

"I was a model man until I met Jack Kriendler and Charlie Berns. I had never missed the 5:42 to Nyack, where I was a member of the Parent-Teacher Association, the Sunnyside Avenue Methodist Episcopal Church, and a property owner. My family and friends and the people at the Nyack bank all trusted me. I had a great belief in myself and a healthy desire to get somewhere.

"Charlie (the four-eyed fellow whose picture you showed me the other day) started me off on beer. When they had me well on that habit, they switched me over to Ballantine's Scotch. I had no reason to distrust them, as they both seemed very friendly, cashing my paychecks every week, even introducing me to people like Gene Fowler and Robert Benchley and Ben Hecht. I will not take up your time about the Hecht matter, as I know that you are a very busy man.

"Well, now I don't know where I stand, excepting that I don't believe I bit George Jean Nathan in the leg the other night. That story comes from Jack. (He is the man with the Shinnecock Hills moustache and the side vents in his coat.) I know that when I asked Benchley how all this could have been prevented, he told me the only danger sign in drinking that *he* knew anything about was when a man has to dogtrot to remain upright going down Fifth Avenue. He had just dogtrotted all the way from the Royalton.

"This statement is free and voluntary, as your rubber hose left no marks."

They loved MacArthur at the bar and once gave him a watch engraved with an iron gate, the "21" symbol, about which MacArthur was supposed to have said, "I paid for this with my left kidney." One night he and Hecht came in for dinner followed by four waiters loaded with trays of food from the Stork Club, claiming that only the drinks were good at "21."

As Samuel Marx says of Hecht and MacArthur, "All descriptions of these two invariably wind up using the word 'irrepressible.' Life was one merry party and they were the life of it at the bar. Ben had turned from writing novels, Charley from plays, and both were luxuriating in the opulent field of screenwriting. Many of the unbelievable stories about this team are true. And many of the believable are not; they created fiction stranger than truth. It's difficult to believe the legend that, while waiting in the great library of banker-philanthropist Otto H. Kahn, they took to autographing most of the collection. If so, there would be a book inscribed, 'To Otto, in loving memory of our weekend at Cape Cod, Emily Brontë.'

"When Charley and Ben were separated for as much as an hour, they rushed back to their corner at '21', where, meeting again, they engaged in rapturous accounts of how they spent the time apart. Once Charley had dropped in on a beauty of the times, Peggy Hopkins Joyce. But Miss Joyce was out, her apartment open. He also found her ice box filled with boxes of Jello, which, he solemnly reported, he dumped into the bathtub, leaving this large portion of stuff to be discovered by Miss Joyce on her return."

Hecht was a verbal brawler in other bars about town, but in the back barroom at "21" he always contained himself, much as did Humphrey Bogart, who was known to be a hell-raiser at mahoganies everywhere but behind the iron gate. That is, except for one occasion when he staged an extremely unattractive scene with his then wife, Mayo Methot, at the bar. Management let it go with nothing more than an admonition to him not to get so emotional in the future.

In the mid-thirties, "21" closed shortly after midnight, a time considered ridiculously early by other places. But Jack & Charlie's emphasis was now on food rather than liquor, a reversal of Prohibition days, and they wished no contretemps with clients or minor skirmishes as often occurred in late-hour clubs. After all, many of the "21" crowd came for lunch, the afternoon, and also dinner, so by midnight it was a long enough day for these regulars. But such people as Hecht and MacArthur were never ready to put the cat out, and Charlie used to have to remind this happy twosome to go home. When that didn't work, he'd turn the lights up high. Finally, he resorted to blinding the colorful team out with spotlights, though it's said they even got used to that. (Interestingly, folks who go to "21" have always had a curious reluctance to go home after dinner, and today Jerry Berns often goes around gently reminding the hangers-on of the late hour.)

Lucius Beebe, whom Wolcott Gibbs once jokingly called the cooking editor of the New York *Herald-Tribune* because Beebe more often than not wrote about wining and dining, reported in his column, "This New York," on February 28, 1936, the cross-section of people found in "21" at that time:

"Seen at lunch at Jack & Charlie's '21': Lawrence Tibbett, very gay; Morris Markey, very professional; the Albert Hinkleys, very Bostonian; Townsend Martin; Dwight Deere Wiman; Ben Hecht and Charley MacArthur, very Hecht and MacArthur; Valerie Ziegler, Mrs. William Randolph Hearst, the Laddie Sanfords; George Marshall, very laundryman; Bill Corum, Dorothy Fell, very severe; Frank Buck, very solvent . . . Lord and Lady Cavendish (they've gone home now) . . . There isn't quite as much hanky waving at '21' as there is at lunch at the Colony these days, but people go there largely to eat, whereas they go to the Colony mainly to see what sort of hat Miss Elsa Maxwell will wear. She has favored the spectators with a series of Alpine sky-pieces reputedly designed by Cecil Beaton and very wonderful, indeed."

Up through the twenties and early thirties, the wealthy who frequented the top speakeasies and then the expensive clubs wore white-tie dress—except, as August ("Gus") Schiavone recalls, on Sundays, when *de rigueur* garb was full riding apparel, most of the chi-chi set being avid Sunday-morning equestrians who, after their fresh-air stints, headed directly to their favorite neighborhood saloon to spend the rest of the day. But then in the mid-thirties, white tie gave way to "tuxedos" and dark suits—that is, except for such sensualists as Lucius Beebe, who never abandoned full formal dress. One of his most colorful excursions "abroad" was when he and his "21" Bowling Team, which starred such celebrities as radio's Ted Husing, and Ben Finney, Gilbert Kahn, Bill Hearst, and towering six-foot-eight-inch Thomas L. Johnson, would dine in the club and then set out to bowl, all in white ties and tails, top hats, walking sticks, and big swooping capes, with Beebe's St. Bernard dog, Bowser, trotting dutifully behind.

It is said that feelings ran high in the middle thirties. If you believed something, you *shouted* it. One shout was the big show that Jack and Charlie mounted in 1936, ushering in a new look for "21." Bulging at the bricks, the establishment was ready to expand into waiting No. 19. Always wanting patrons to be part of any "family action"—an attitude that was one of "21's" drawing cards—Jack and Charlie sent out New Year's greetings announcing "We are breaking through to '19' 36," and they staged an "in-house bash," a night called the "Breaking Thru Party." A group of regulars had been asked to wait in the barroom until the run of customers had gone. Then, under the leadership of Dudley Field Malone, a famous divorce attorney, the men were positioned and directed to *push*.

The temporary partition between the buildings yielded to bring into being the brand-new adjacent room, or the middle section of the barroom as we know it today. Since this bigger room gave more space for thirsty barflies, the mahogany on the northwest corner of No. 21 gave way to a larger, semicircular one on the west wall.

When bartender Bill Darcy, while tending his glasses, would lean back against the back-bar cabinets, as all bartenders seem to do, he would sometimes almost fall down. Everyone thought it was because he couldn't get used to his big new "home," but some of

the help knew that it was because Bill's ubiquitous glass of water was really gin.

Expansion of the premises made enough new space available on the third floor for Jack to design himself a bigger bachelor flat. (Charlie, who had once lived over the shop, now resided uptown with his wife, Molly.) There were also extra rooms in which friends could congregate to play backgammon, checkers and chess, cards and dominoes, or to do crossword puzzles—a passion of Jack's and of the era—and drink a little cognac. All this was a nostalgic reflection back to the friendly Village days when such games whiled away many an hour. Employees also sometimes slept in the extra space, and as Johnny Seeman recalls, "We used to pack eighteen into one room in No. 19, before anyone even knew we owned it." One of the eighteen was "Crown Prince" Mike Romanoff, who was then in his lean and hungry days, newly arrived, it is said, from Brooklyn!

The club stayed open during the alterations, and work went on right through meal-times, with thunderous crashes and impassioned language occasionally wafting from behind the plasterboard partitions. Everyone seemed to enjoy the activity, which was described by one patron as rather like Paris during the siege.

After the club's enlargement a monstrous air-conditioning system was installed, the first in any top-rated New York restaurant. Jack was extremely proud of this feature, and one blistering July day it was turned on for the first time. Machinery whirred, patrons waited, and air currents began to circulate about the house.

"Refreshing, isn't it?" beamed Jack. Everyone agreed that it was just splendid, all the while mopping their faces with napkins, handkerchiefs, and everything but the table-cloths. Streams of sweat poured down the wealthiest of necks; the temperature went not down but up, up, up. "Just wait until it starts to really work," advised Jack. Finally abandoning all hope, Bert Lahr streaked for the door. "I'm going up to the steam room at the Athletic Club to cool off," he shrieked. Someone had mistakenly set the cooling system on "hot" instead of "cool," and for months patrons remarked venomously to the partners: "Refreshing, isn't it?"

Left, Fifty-second Street: from Swing Street in the thirties to "Stripty-second Street" in the forties, so called because of the number of strip-tease clubs. Below, the new west-wall bar at "21"

8

All in

the

Family

With expansion of the club, and its remarkable ability to attract the same people week in and week out—a heritage carried over to this day—Jack and Mac needed management reinforcements, so they called into their business their younger brothers, I. Robert ("Bob") and H. Peter ("Pete"), and also H. Jerome ("Jerry") Berns, Charlie's younger brother. All were college graduates, but taskmaster Jack, who wanted to keep the house *en famille*, made them start their restaurant careers the hard way, through the kitchen. Bob once recalled when he went into the club in 1936, just out of Rutgers:

"I started as a scullery boy, and that meant working in the basement up to my knees in plucking chickens, scraping vegetables, scaling fish, and doing all the drudgery you go through to learn the bottom-to-top operation of a restaurant . . . but it was where I learned a true appreciation for fresher than fresh foods, the very soul of any great kitchen.

"Shortly after coming into the club," Bob continued, "I got a message that Mr. Jack wanted to see me—we were all called by Mr. 'first-name,' there being three of us Kriendlers in the house. Putting on my coat and tie, I went upstairs. My brother said, 'I have an important assignment. Gene Fowler, the author, is in the hospital and is desperate for some Scotch. Take a bottle up to him but don't let his doctors or nurses see you.' I was interested in the contemporary novel, and in the few months that I had been downstairs I had heard about John O'Hara, Sinclair Lewis, Ben Hecht, Budd Schulberg, Somerset Maugham, H. G. Wells, Robert Sherwood, and all the famous authors who ate upstairs—*verboten* territory to me. So I had never met, let alone laid eyes on any of these prominent men. I raced across the street to the Drama Bookshop, got a copy of Fowler's *Salute to Yesterday*, had it wrapped together with a bottle of Ballantine's, and hopping into a cab, I went shaking with excitement up to Doctors Hospital.

"When I got to Fowler's room, he sent the private nurse out and hid the bottle under the blanket. I asked him if he'd inscribe my book, and he wrote: 'To my timely young friend, who rushed into the battle with a bottle and thereby saved a life.'

"By 1938 I had been promoted to the floor upstairs, and was well into collecting autographs. Now I was as excited as hell, because I could meet John Steinbeck and Ernest Hemingway and all the writers. One day I had a copy of *The Grapes of Wrath* and asked Hemingway—he was by now like a father to me—if Steinbeck would inscribe the book. Steinbeck was known to be very difficult to approach. Steinbeck balked, even though Hemingway insisted. 'I don't like to sign books,' Steinbeck said, 'what should I say?' Hemingway told him to say something

scatological. So my inscription reads: 'To Bob Kriendler, Scatologically, John Steinbeck.' There was a drawing under his name of a little bird in flight, which seemed to appear on many of Steinbeck's inscriptions.

"Several years later, when an anthology of his writings came out, Steinbeck answered my request for his autograph in *Portable Steinbeck* by writing: 'Bob—It's a little tiny world as we both know—*pas de merde*. John Steinbeck."

In the mid-thirties the club began to stock current best sellers by the club's customers at the tobacco counter in the lobby, a custom that is carried on to this day. The story goes that one day in the late thirties after sports writer Paul Gallico had written *Farewell to Sport*, he was lunching at "21" and other patrons bought up all the copies and rushed on the author for autographs. One cynical friend, watching the onslaught,

At left, Mr. Pete, Mr. Bob, Mr. Jack, Mr. Mac. Below, Luisa and Jack's wedding, Miami, 1940, with Pete, Lota and husband Mac, and Marine Bob

during which Gallico grew so confused he tried to sign books with his fork and eat asparagus with his fountain pen, sent him the following note: "Do you regard this as proof that the people who eat here can also read and write?"

Bob's collection of autographed books numbered in the hundreds, and among the many humorous inscriptions are such as Robert Ruark wrote in *Something of Value*: "For Robert, the clean, upstanding and heroic one —if a little queer, Love, Bob." Another inscription reads: "To Robert Kriendler, W. Somerset Maugham makes his name at the 21 on January 16, 1939." And in *The Man Who Came to Dinner*: "For Bob, in memory of those lustfilled nights when first we lay in each other's arms and tasted the sweetness of sin, Moss Hart." And underneath: "Me neither, George S. Kaufman." When Bob first realized his love for books and started collecting—a passion that once prompted John Steinbeck to pen, "He is the author of several volumes—*Bee Finding 1936; Bee Keeping 1937; Bee Losing 1937½*"—he always had two books inscribed, keeping one and sending the other to the Rutgers University Library, where the books formed the Jack Kriendler Memorial Collection. Here one found tomes by such names as Ludwig Bemelmans, Stephen Vincent Benét, Dwight D. Eisenhower, Jim Farley, Rebecca West, Ellery Queen, and Morris Ernst, and contemporaries Eleanor Harris, Alan King, A. E. Hotchner, Art Buchwald, Melvin M. Belli, Fleur Cowles, Arlene Francis, and Benjamin A. Javits.

During the dark days of Prohibition, Jerry Berns's mother had sent him out of town to the University of Cincinnati to get him away from the lure of the speakeasy business. A city boy who had never seen many trees other than those in Central Park —"our backyard," he once said, "the one we gave to the city"—Jerry found the Ohio River country to his liking, and after gradua-

tion stayed on to become drama and film critic of the *Cincinnati Enquirer*. But in 1938 the call of the tamed and famed "21" brought him back to Manhattan and the club, where he started as a steward.

And along came Pete Kriendler, graduate of Saint Lawrence University in 1929, selling off his seat on the New York Curb Exchange —now the American Stock Exchange—for, as the rumor went, $258,000 over the $26,000 Jack paid to buy it for him.

In 1940, Jack countered the all-male "21" household by marrying Baroness Luisa Du-

Bob marries Florence Feller in 1937

mont de Chassart, a truly beautiful Italian woman and a fine queen for King Jack. The road to marriage was not all smooth, for he practically had to take on dueling bouts with the Baroness's husband, a Belgian Count, who was not about to relinquish his wife to "Two-Trigger Jack," who nevertheless turned out to be faster on the draw. Divorced in Florida, the Baroness finally became Mrs.

John Carl Kriendler, and the Count found himself a new wife, declaring that "now we all can be happy." Jack and Luisa moved into a baroque apartment over the club with cupids dancing on the ceiling and Jack and Luisa dancing on the floor—when they weren't entertaining downstairs in the club.

It was said that "Nobody with a million dollars could bore 'Two-Trigger Jack' and nobody with less than a million could interest him." This city cowhand met his match one Christmas Eve just before World War II. A light snow was falling, and Jack, the romantic, decided to put a table and chairs outside the club in the little courtyard between the front door and the iron gate and have a drink out in the snow. George Jean Nathan joined him, and the men, snug in fur coats, sat gathering snowflakes and drinking cognac. Along came a lassie and four Salvation Army musicians, who paused and then began to play Christmas carols. They were the only ones passing by who didn't raise an eyebrow at this holiday odd-couple, and Jack was so impressed that he asked the shivering Army into the club to play in the barroom. Surprisingly, the glittering patrons were touched, and sizable tips moistened with millionaires' tears were collected by the lassie, after which Jack further startled the musicians by treating them to dinner. So a tradition began. For close to four decades, the Salvation Army has sung and supped in the club at Christmastime, doing several performances a season, often aided by the charitable voices of Bing Crosby and Lanny Ross.

No other restaurant in New York has held such emotional attachment at holiday time as "21," whose clients would not dream of letting a season go by without dropping into the club to enjoy a drink at the bar, kiss and shake hands all around, and lift songs and salutes to Christmas and a good and prosperous new year.

The house used to be open on Thanksgiving, Christmas, and New Year's Day because

Jack believed they should create a "home" for regulars who could not be with their families. In 1938, he inaugurated the famous Christmas Day Lonely Hearts' Dinner, attended over the years by celebrities from all walks of life. Though now closed on major holidays, New Year's Eve at "21" is still a tradition for regulars who gather at the club, most at their very own preferred tables, to sip bottles of Dom Pérignon and Louis Roederer Cristal (a champagne made popular at "21") and to sup in style. Just before midnight, the help comes charging through the restaurant banging with wooden spoons on

Charlie with younger brother Jerry

shiny copper pots and pans to help force out the birth of a new year.

At the slightest provocation, real or imagined, Jack, a "celebrant" for any cause, used to throw corned beef and cabbage parties in the private rooms above the club. He would celebrate his own return from a jaunt down cowboy way . . . his birthday . . . Charlie and Molly's anniversary . . . a house member's

93

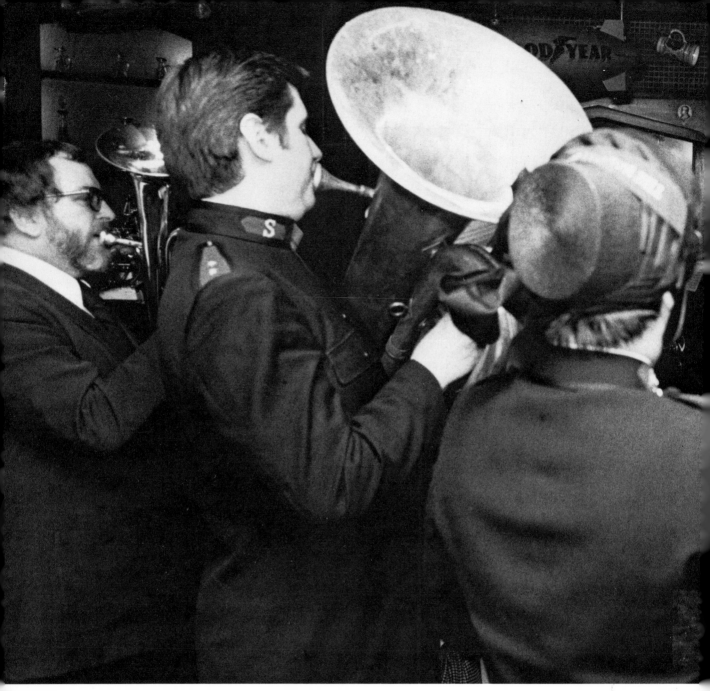

return from a safari to some far-flung place ... a promotion ... a birth ... even a divorce. (After Franchot Tone and Joan Crawford were divorced, they came into "21" to toast one another with champagne.)

Jack showed his appreciation to the Yale men who stayed loyal to the club during the Depression and after Repeal by hosting two annual dinners, one called "Ben Quinn's Kitchen," held on the second floor, where there was a taproom-cum-Yale-fraternity

room for private parties. As Quinn recalls, "It was always a fine banquet for about twenty-five men ... it became such a festive occasion that as we became older our constitutions could not take such festivities, even once a year, so the custom was discontinued."

The other affair was for a group of Yale graduates and undergraduates called the "Comanche Club," a wing-ding that included the best possible meal the house could pro-

duce, as well as all the necessary wines and spirits. As sports commentator and writer Bob Cooke remembers, "I invited a classmate named Richard E. Moore, who later became a special assistant to President Nixon. Moore, perhaps the most brilliant man in the class of Yale '36, couldn't believe that Jack would spend all that money on a free dinner just for a group of New Haven men, and he said, 'I'll bet he never does that again.' The bet was covered and Moore lost, because the follow-ing year Jack outdid himself at the annual Comanche banquet. Finally Moore was given an explanation for Jack's generosity: The guests were hand-picked, all members of The Fence Club, a Yale fraternity that pro-duced mostly millionaires, and for the price of one dinner each year Jack created lifetime customers, all of whom had more substantial

Singer Lanny Ross leads the Salvation Army's annual Christmas performance in the barroom at "21"

credit than Dun & Bradstreet."

Although Jack created a home for those people he liked, on the other hand he extended an icy arm of hospitality to those he disliked. Writer George Frazier once told two stories epitomizing Jack's firmness about picking his customers the way he picked his friends. It seems that on one occasion Jack stepped up to Frank Costello and said, "I hope you won't take this wrong, Mr. Costello, but I don't think this is the sort of place for you." Costello raged and swore he'd close the place. But instead, his mania for respectability led him to spread the story that he had designed the electronically controlled bar of "21's" speakeasy days. Just before World War II, Jack once approached Congressman Hamilton Fish, Sr., a "super" champion of American isolationism, as Fish was leaving "21." As Frazier told the story, Jack said, "Mr. Fish, I'm afraid that I don't like either you or your politics. I, personally, would appreciate your not coming in here again."

During the early forties, while war raged round the world and sophisticated New York was as homespun as any small town in Kansas, there grew up a whole new category of "21" stories. A socialite once sat in the lobby of the club selling one-dollar tickets to a benefit for camp shows. "21" was money territory, and many habitués passing through the lobby took fifty to a hundred dollars' worth. An army private came in, handed the socialite a hundred-dollar bill, and the lady gave him back ninety-nine dollars, hating to take any more from a twenty-one-dollar-a-month man. Just as she was handing him the change, insisting he should *not* buy more tickets, he insisting he wanted to, the maître d' slid up and whispered softly, "Your table is ready, Mr. Rockefeller."

Lieutenant Putnam Humphreys, on the eve of his departure for active service, and sportscaster Paul Douglas stood at the bar drinking, and a lady came in and said, "May I join you—just one drink—for old time's sake?" All three drank a toast. The lady, Gerry Higgins, had been married to both.

On another occasion, such diverse figures as writer Lillian Hellman, former ambassador Joseph P. Kennedy, back from his ambassadorship to the Court of St. James's, actor William Powell, and banking tycoon Emory Buckner stood at the bar listening to an FDR speech on the bar radio. While F. B. Davis, head of U.S. Rubber, and Vincent P. Dole of the pineapple clan drank next to polo player Winston Guest and actor Errol Flynn, Guest, who would later become a distinguished Marine, said, "I'd like to serve under you, Errol; you always seem to come out of every battle so well . . . even when they bump you off you are still around the next day."

With husbands, beaux, and lovers gone off to war, there were tables and tables of women at "21," and the "ladies' lunch" came into vogue. For the first time, they were allowed to lunch in the barroom and in the upstairs dining rooms without escorts. Over too many martinis, these girls pretended to be jolly, but you could see on many of their faces those tight, unpleasant expressions that well-to-do women without men so often wear in public.

But not so for bulky Elsa Maxwell, who frequented "21" with gaudily grand Lucius Beebe in tow—both of them institutions like the opera or the circus, and both collecting house menus to mail to their friends in the trenches, on battleships, and in the air. Many of the guys said later that this kindness speeded up the war effort because it gave them impetus to get that foot back on the bar rail at "21."

Jack, a retired major in the United States Marine Corps Reserves, and Jerry and Pete stayed on Fifty-second Street during World War II, while Bob and Mac went off to active duty. Bob spent thirty months in the Marines in the South Pacific theater, where he would have Scotch and food shipped out to him from "21" delivered by regulars of the club who had been on leave and returned to that war theater. Dean Quimby, of Rochester, an old "21-er," once told the story of the time he was in the Pacific on a cruiser that was shot up. When they got into port he discovered that Bob was in the outfit, and Bob shortly came to greet him saying, "Look what I have to share with you, Dean, a tin of fresh caviar from '21.'"

"Well, I did have a pretty good larder," Bob once recalled, "You see, when Gil Kahn went off the island of Guadalcanal, where I was, he had a footlocker full of goodies from '21': Beluga caviar, shad roe, smoked salmon, oysters, and *pâté* and such, and he gave me his entire pantry. Incidentally, he had kept it in his tent, which was identified by a big sign saying '21.' I shared my bounty with fellow islanders, then Majors Malcolm K. Beyer, Martin Fenton, and George Percy, some of the guys who helped make that island tolerable."

Bob, in fact, was in a whole mess of wars, being a veteran of the Korean War as well and of an active duty tour in Vietnam. During World War II he received, among many awards, the Purple Heart, the Legion of Merit, and the Bronze Star.

Mac went to London with the Eighth Air Force, serving as a lieutenant colonel. When discharged in 1945, he was Chief of Management Control, Eastern District, Air Technical

Captain Robert Kriendler,
New River, North Carolina, 1942

Above, annual Comanche dinner. Below, Francis T. Hunter, Bill Hardey, Mac, Charlie, Julius Hallheimer, and Jack (left to right, back row), with Jane Hunter, Evelyn Hardey, Lota, Molly, and Luisa

Mac and chef Ploneis greet C. R. Smith, president of American Airlines, financier Bernard Baruch, center, and Alfred T. Wadsworth, left, editor of the Manchester *Guardian*

Service Command. He received the Exceptional Service Award, the highest civilian decoration of the Air Force, the Legion of Merit, and the Air Force Commendation Medal. With friends, he formed the Iron Gate Chapter of "Air Alumni."

Back at the "21" bar at closing time one very rainy night during the war, Robert Benchley asked the uniformed man at the door to call him a cab, whereupon the man drew himself up to full height and said, "Sir, I am an admiral in the United States Navy." Benchley quickly replied, "Good, call me a boat."

Another long night at the bar saw Benchley step out the front door to Fifty-second Street and come charging quickly back. He was as ashen and limp as gray flannel and badly in need of a double brandy, telling Mac that the street was filled with elephants. "They were marching silently down the street," said Benchley. After calming him, Mac looked out, saw nothing, and returned to the bar. The next day Mac had to admit Benchley had been right. In the papers were photos of the Ringling Brothers and Barnum & Bailey Circus moving their elephants

across town the night before, and they had moved quietly because, as the paper said, the bullhands had bound each elephant's foot in burlap to avoid making noise crossing the midtown streets on the way to Madison Square Garden.

Benchley's quips at the "21" bar have been told and retold. It was there during a discussion about playwright Robert E. Sherwood, a man six feet eight inches tall, that Benchley leaped up onto a chair, extended his arm at shoulder height, and said, "I've known Bob Sherwood since he was this high."

Sheldon Tannen with wife, Ellen

Mary Martin and Jerry Berns

Benchley's loyalty to "21" culminated with a memorial service to him at the club after his death in 1945. Friends had gathered and braced themselves with plenty of Scotch, and at 6:00 p.m., in a private room upstairs, Marc Connelly, who was in charge of the group, made a call to Hollywood to Dorothy Parker, who had agreed to hold a simultaneous memorial on the Coast for her long-time friend. "We're here," Connelly told Parker. "Now, Dottie, if you all will raise your glasses . . ."

Parker cut him off with an astonished, "Raise our glasses . . . why Marc, you stupid bastard, it's only three o'clock here, and we're all at work. I told you to have the service at 6:00 p.m. I meant *West Coast time,* you silly son of a bitch."

A brass plaque to Benchley's memory in the bar simply says, "Robert Benchley—His Corner." There, Benchley once sat watching John O'Hara buttoning up his many-buttoned tweed jacket all the way to the top button. Benchley called, "Stop, John. You'll cut off your circulation."

In the late forties the personal reign of Jack and Charlie came to an end. Jack died of a coronary thrombosis on August 13, 1947, in his flat above the restaurant. Only forty-nine years old, he left an estate valued at some one million dollars. He also left a thriving club, and a puzzle that lasted for eight years: More than $180,000 in cash was found in his safety-deposit box. Nobody knew what the money was for, but someone finally figured out that these were the funds that Jack had set aside to cash checks for customers. Whatever the purpose, this cash supply was one of the obstructions to settling Jack's estate, and delayed passing ownership of the club on to his heirs.

Jack was a keen executive, and he had built a fine restaurant that ranked with the few other select old-guard gastronomic establishments of post-Prohibition New York

Gene Cavallero's old Colony, Henri Soulé's Le Pavillon, Roger Chauveron's Café Chambord (later the Café Chauveron). And though Jack is still spoken about as one of our most unique restaurateurs of this century, he was also just a great guy to most who knew him. Personally, he was a legend of heroic proportions, and for a while Hollywood considered making a movie based on his life—undoubtedly it would have been directed by the likes of Erich Von Stroheim! As Bill Corum said of the debonair Jack: "For me there will never be another host in a public place like my friend Jack. Not only because I liked him and know that the feeling was mutual, which is true, but also because he had the knack, somehow, of making me feel that a party was afoot. That we were conniving a little together toward the goal of a good time. Or, as my grandmother used to say it, of putting the big pot in the little one.

"It is not an easy thing to explain . . . it was a feeling; a reaction to a personality. Suppose I just say that Jack made living in this town more fun."

Ward Morehouse immortalized Jack's inordinately generous character with an anecdote to bring him a bit more closely into focus: "He showed me, in his upstairs apartment one afternoon, a cowboy outfit that he intended wearing on one of his trips to the Great Southwest. I admired the get-up immensely. The next day Jack's tailor called upon me . . . within two weeks delivered to me apparel, including boots, spurs, and hat, that would have made me the best-dressed plainsman in all Montana. I got into those Western togs and asked the valet of my hotel to come up and look me over. 'Well,' he said after a few minutes of inspection, 'if I were you I'd never take those things off. They're better than any clothes you ever owned.'"

Although no one would believe that Jack's zany voice booming "Empty Saddles in the Old Corral" (his favorite cowboy song) would no longer echo through "21,"

and for a while the house spirit was truly dashed, before anyone realized what was happening brothers Bob, Pete, and Mac, and cousin Jerry, now grown-up "picolos" (fetch-and-carry restaurant "apprentices") and well indoctrinated in theories on how Jack ran his saloon of fine food, drink, and public service, stepped in to fill Jack's shoes. And as the big-brother helping hand, there was Charlie right next door in the Brands. Mac became president of the club, until he later went over to the Brands with Charlie, at which point Bob followed as president; Pete became managing director, and Jerry corporate vice president and secretary.

Robert Benchley, the true man-about-town: at lunch he's at "21," at 5:00 p.m. he's at "21," and at 11:00 p.m. he's at "21"

Mac was a sweetheart of a man, soft and kind. He didn't put on airs and he didn't take the social whirl too seriously. His credo was to roll through life and live it the best way he could manage—though it was generally agreed that Mac lived it remarkably well. Ulric Bell once called Mac "an entrepreneur of fun and freedom, a guy who works from the top down, swearing at the stuffed shirt and reducing him to the common level (and not merely by the economic attrition of '21's' prodigious rum and bar checks) . . . he exudes a contempt for the synthetic genius, the tinsel titan and the dollar patriot."

Like Jack, Mac had eyes for gals with well-turned ankles. His old expatriate friend Anthony Paget, Jr., recalls the time Mac arrived in Madrid, newly married, and called Tony. "Hey, Tony," Mac said, "meet me in the hotel bar and bring a couple gorgeous *guapas* and we'll do the town." Taken aback, Tony said, "But Mac, aren't you just married . . . on your honeymoon, where's the bride?" Mac gasped and said, "Oh Lord, I forgot—she's upstairs."

Just before Jack's death, Kriendler nephew Sheldon Jay Tannen (son of Anna and Henry), a World War II veteran and student at New York University, joined "21," eventually to assume the position of vice president. He was knowledgeable in the restaurant business, having apprenticed with his father and Bill Hardey in Bill's Gay Nineties. Thinking that Sheldon did not have the proper carriage for a restaurateur, Jack bought a surgical shoulder brace for him, which Sheldon wore until Jack decided that he properly hung his weight from his shoulders and stood erect as a colonel. When asked why he would tolerate this quirk of

Left, Gus Lux with a "21" pièce de résistance. Above, "21" staff circa 1950, left to right:
René Chapelard, sommelier; Philip Caselli, maître d'hôtel; Gus Lux, steward; Monte Sideman, receptionist; Charles Sercus, chief steward; Vincent Fasolo, bar captain; Emil Bernasconi, head bartender; Hubert Walsh, chief cashier; Henry Zbikiewicz, bartender; Remo Revel, headwaiter, bar; Pierre Pastre, headwaiter; T. Mario Ricci, sommelier; Jimmie Collins, receptionist, and Yves Ploneis, chef

Jack's, Sheldon answered: "We know how to separate family love from business."

Although the gin mill at No. 21 West Fifty-second Street will never for many people lose its identity as "Jack & Charlie's '21,'" a metamorphosis of the name was inevitable once burghers Jack and Charlie had gone. Shortly after Jack's heirs took over, they formed a corporation called "The '21' Club, Inc." and as the world began to live by numbers, the house name was shortened, in common vernacular, to just "21," the name Jack and Charlie personally used for this famous house. It must be known, however, that such a house of pleasure has always had many pet names among its habitués. For instance, Mrs. David Morse calls it "The Cradle," since she was born (as a Hochstadter) in townhouse No. 21. To others it's affectionately known as "the numbers"—two plus one, or simply "The Three," a name that's also appropriate in terms of the house itself. When "21" Brands, Inc. moved out of No. 17, the club took over that property, expanding again, in 1945, to embrace three townhouses, the space that "21" occupies today.

Apart from the changes of proprietors and name, the close of the forties also witnessed the end of the "golden" people in "21." That was a group so chummy that the "21-ers" would challenge the Club 18-ers across Fifty-second Street to snowball duels. Inside the walls, Ernest Hemingway took the hospitality so much to heart that one night as he was escorting his lady friend up the stairs, passion overcame him on the landing and he became the protagonist in a colorful tale of his own which has long been told along the bar in "21."

Glittering Café Society was fading. It had always lived by feeding on figments of gossip anyway, and during the war years when there were bigger issues in the news, a disrupted society had not found time to ponder seriously over idle and frivolous activities of the rich and relaxed. When the fifties hit, bringing the great age of television, with starlets moving from West Coast film sets to New York TV studios, executives following their money-makers east, and all people traveling the globe and bringing a bigger, more international world to New York, "21" became dominated not by the monied social clientele nor the literati, but by the expense-account crowd, a wide spectrum of communications people, celebrities, business executives, publicists, and press agents.

These people of the Age of the Expense Account spent money at "21" like button-down sailors on leave, pouring wine like water, eating caviar like crackers, and dining on nine varieties of oysters and whatever game might be in season, which sometimes included Scotch grouse flown in by Pan Am. Bar jokes turned from talk of the antics of tall, bearded, and dignified Monty Woolley —who was known to bend over and stick several packages of matches under Mac Kriendler's shoe, light them all, then stand back and squeal with delight as Mac screamed—to tall tales about expense accounts. One of the funniest of that era concerns "21" regular Gene Fowler. It seems that he was sent to northern Canada to locate some lost aviators, and in the process spent some three thousand dollars. Back in New York, with no recall of how he spent it, he invented the purchase of a mythical dog team, then the mythical illness of a dog, making medical attention necessary. To end his story, the dog died and he charged off the dog's funeral, accounting for each item to the final sixty dollars: "Flowers for bereft bitch, $60."

A tourist in the club at this time would have rubbed elbows with Edward R. Murrow, the intelligence of television, Marlene Dietrich, Lilli Palmer and Rex Harrison, Prince Rainier courting Grace Kelly, Henry Fonda and Mary Martin, the waist-clinched Gabor sisters and Mama (this a glittering group once called "Goldirocks and the Three Bears"), and epicurean film wizard Alfred Hitchcock, who once reversed his meal by having ice cream first and steak last. The women of Café Society who had never broken a nail over lifting a pencil gave way to glamorous working women such as Betty Furness and Faye Emerson, who had a TV show on CBS-TV. And—hold your hat—famous madam Polly Adler, who had a party at "21" for her book, *A House Is Not a Home.* When the club was asked if Miss Adler could have her party there, Jerry Berns said, "Why not? Where else would she go?" After all, as Jerry now recalls, "She had a business arrangement with us; we sold her whisky and if someone was looking for entertainment he was referred to Miss Adler."

Private parties of every sort became part of the "21" life style. The banquet department had featured in the forties such exten-

sive grape and grouse work as a ten-course Continental repast—from caviar blinis through partridge and *sorbet*, a chestnut purée, complete with eight wines. This commemorated the thirteenth anniversary of "The Big Six" at Jack & Charlie's, on December 12, 1946 (the guests being Charles Berns, Francis T. Hunter, David Katz, Jack and Mac Kriendler, and William Samuel Zinman). Now it moved with the times to offer in the fifties a six-course, five-wine meal including smoked salmon, fillet, and ice-cream cake, as tendered for the National League on its seventy-fifth anniversary to honor Ford Christopher Frick as the Commissioner of Baseball. By the seventies, the club's catering service came to offer such contemporary dinners as the Spanish celebration with gazpacho, roast pig, and Rioja wine, *una Fiesta para Celebrar El Aniversario vigésimo quinto de las Nupcias de Ricardo y Jane* (Colonel Richard and Jane Stark), December 20, 1972.

Pete, Mac, and Bob in Bermuda, 1964

9

Home-Away-from-Home

Jimmy Cannon was in Toots Shor's a few years ago when he and his friends saw a man come in who looked like Spencer Tracy. When the Cannon crowd found out it wasn't Tracy, one of them said, "Everyone who comes in here looks like someone famous." To which Cannon replied, "Yes, and the people they look like go to '21.'"

This house, the nerve center of New York's social intrigue and a place with a savory and authentic scent of power, is where the men's-room attendant is rumored to make some fifty thousand dollars a year just for smiling and being polite (as one regular of the club jokingly says, "I can eat in just about any other restaurant for what it costs me in the men's room at '21'").

Here Dr. and Mrs. Kissinger stop by when they have the time, and Sir Brian Cheesman entertains with, so the Palm Beach story goes, fourteen thousand bucks' worth of champagne a week. Christopher Cerf stops by to check out his private cellar of Chambertin Clos de Béze, and Vice President Nelson A. Rockefeller makes a special trip to the dining room when the management calls to say that the first whitebait of the season is ready for him, or that the oyster crabs have come in. Executive James Gillon drops by daily for Chicken Hash "21," and businessman "Hubie" Boscowitz comes daily to eat only scallops for lunch, a habit since Prohibition days, while columnist Louis Sobol comes to take only chicken.

Presidents Truman, Eisenhower, Kennedy, Johnson, Nixon, and Ford have been fed at "21," at what one person calls more or less a "dollar a bite," and this great private preserve is where former Chief of Protocol and Mrs. Emil ("Bus") Mosbacher, Jr., were once hosted by President Nixon. In this plush and exclusive house dine Helen Hayes and

Truman Capote, the Shah of Iran, H.I.H. Prince Abdorreza Pahlavi, the Shah's brother, and bird-shooting pal Franc Ricciardi, and designers John Weitz and Bonnie Cashin. There are special tables for the Sulzbergers, Toppings, Sarnoffs, Forbeses, Farleys, and O'Brians. And Jackie O dines in the club's upstairs dining room while sister Lee sups downstairs in the bar.

Few tourists drop into "21," for few have the requisite nerves of steel to push across

space at the curb, and the frequent hordes of autograph hunters on the sidewalk, of such persistence that Humphrey Bogart once came out snarling, "Commit insecticide."

Two steps leading down from the front sidewalk and over a door mat emblazoned with "21" bring you to the set of glass entrance doors (the speakeasy "iron doors" redesigned by Chuck Luckman in 1952) leading through a narrow foyer to another set of doors opening into the lobby of "21." Here, on the right at a desk, is the *Guardia Civil*—

Pete and Bob greet President John F. Kennedy

Chuck Anderson: He knows who can come into "21"

the famous portals, guarded by the legendary iron gate and by an eye-catching lineup of cast-iron jockeys wearing the racing colors of American thoroughbred stables, owned by turf-minded patrons—folks from Alfred Gwynne Vanderbilt to George Widener to Lucille and Gene Markey (the order is periodically changed so no one name stays first or last too long). These colorful fellows can tell one at a glance that something special must be inside. But the biggest clue during business hours is the limousines that vie for

not real local police, of course, but Chuck Anderson and Monte Sideman, twin guardians of the famous front door, assisted by Michael Bemer and Tom Ray, who, in 1975, started "apprenticing" the portal protection. But they aren't simply doormen. Monte, once married to Bea Kriendler and at "21" since 1935, and Chuck, a supple former tennis champion who came in 1955 (when Jimmie retired), and Michael and Tom, are actually receptionists, or "screeners." They are part of the management of happiness and decorum, ever watchful for the likes of Zap Comix characters in clodhoppers who might truck in unannounced to do a little dawdling and dust up the place. Legally, "21" is a public restaurant and, as Jerry Berns says, "We are glad to welcome any strangers, so long as there is available space."

Crashing the gate, a term reminiscent of speakeasy days when folks got in who were really unwanted, is not hard, but it's more a matter of whether you feel or know you belong. Howard Hughes of old was self-assured some of whom have frequented "21" since the day it opened, there are truly no agreed-upon rules for what makes people acceptable or not. Money and name, social position and fame are helpful, but a junior executive may be welcomed while his rich boss is an outsider. Even the *Social Register* is no longer a checkpoint, for being dropped from its ranks has sometimes been cause for lively celebration parties.

Chuck and Monte have been known to turn away dozens of people a day not only

"Punch" Sulzberger, right, with Florence and Bob and a friend

enough to arrive in sneakers and a taxi, leave the cab door wide open and ask the doorman to pay the fare, swoop into the club and order up all kinds of goodies, then, as the story goes, disappear without even paying back the doorman. Helen Griffith, society writer for the Sarasota *Herald*, reports that Rocky Graziano once quipped after having dinner at the club, "Can you imagine them letting me into '21'? I'm lucky to count that high."

Except for the core of dedicated regulars, because the house is truly filled to capacity, but because the people at the door are breaking one of the house rules, such as arriving with too much hooch already under the belt or wearing the wrong kind of clothes. Other reasons may be less tangible. As Chuck says, "They are people I don't know so why should I be friendly to them?" Or they may be "not our kind of people," a turn-away excuse Jack started years ago.

Monte remembers an incident when an elderly man and his wife came in for lunch

one Saturday after having called for a reservation. Jack did not like older people in his house, since he wanted only young bodies to dress the room, and he gave Monte a finger in the back meaning "Let them wait and get them out." The couple waited two hours and then left. The next Monday, the man, a vice president of a large steel company, requested an appointment to discuss the matter with Jack, who agreed to the meeting but kept him waiting for at least an hour anyway. When Jack saw the man, he gave him a card

with an initialed okay and said, "It won't happen again, just present this card." The gentleman left, and Jack turned to Monte and said, "Make it difficult for him the next time he comes in."

In the early days, nobody would go to the club without calling first, even if he was just planning a round at the bar. If a newcomer reserved and came in looking like a no-no, he was told "We thought you made the reservation for tomorrow; sorry, we're full."

The autocratic nature of the club's door

policy has given rise to many jokes. For example, artist Rube Goldberg, satirist of the technological age, invented a machine for getting into "21": "Live seal (A) balances ball (B) and applauds himself, causing string (C) to shoot bone (D) from pistol (E)—bone lands on platform (F)—dog (G) bends head to pick up bone, causing candle (H) to set off bomb (I) and blow up the joint!"

"21" has never refused admittance to anyone who might "dress up" the place or en-

hance its glamour or prestige. Monte tells the story of the day Lord Snowden came in, and though no one knew him, Monte decided that this chap's upper-crust English accent had to mean that he was okay. But of course these receptionists, who probably know more of the famous faces of the world than any other two people except Jack and Charlie in the old days, have been known to err. One story goes back to when the famous photographer Robert Capa got off a plane, unshaven and rumpled, and waggled straight to "21" to moisten his throat. He went unrecognized at the door and was asked, "Do you have a reservation?"—the formidable question that is usually thrust out to halt an undesirable. Capa retorted, "Oh no, but I'm here to meet Robert Capa, the photographer." He was swept in with open arms.

Women get a frown if they wear clothes that are too revealing, or in bad taste. But *whose* taste? During the thirties, Katharine Hepburn was admitted in slacks, but that was the only counterculture attire to invade the premises until close to thirty years later when the club finally relaxed its rules and let women wear trousers—after all, clubby "21" prides itself on being the quintessence of masculinity. But beauty is beauty. Stanley B. Tracy, of Summit, New Jersey, once wrote to "21" saying that a table adjacent to his was occupied by Ingrid Bergman and two gentlemen and "we could not help but overhear their conversation, which dealt with the financing of some sort of casino in Cairo . . . fascinating, but more so was Bergman, attired in sweater, tweed skirt, and with no makeup. We all voted her a regular and the best-looking woman in the room."

Lack of a necktie will keep any man out of the club—Sammy Davis once took a tie from Chuck and knotted it around his head. And Groucho Marx took—with annoyance—a house tie to put on over his Groucho T-shirt and later tried to get everyone in the dining room to remove their ties. No one did. However, exceptions were made. Rudolf Nureyev was the first man allowed in without a jacket, the management saying, "We realize that Mr. Nureyev *is* different," and Marc Chagall is welcomed into the club in slacks and a plaid shirt, so long as he gives his menu order in the form of a sketch to Pete Kriendler, who in turn makes sure that Chagall receives no check. Joan Miró has inscribed menus for the house, but it is said that he pays his own way.

"21" is not a place for handout hospitality. As Mark Hellinger once said, "I hadn't been sitting in their place more than fourteen hours when the house bought a drink. I cannot forget that occasion, because it has never happened since." John Steinbeck once said of Marine Bob Kriendler, "He did not lead the charge of San Juan Hill, but that does not mean there will be no charge." Jack's philosophy was that "If it's given away it can't be sold," and as Jack used to emphasize, "I don't mean just whisky."

Though it's said that one should be a frequent and big spender to be welcomed any time in this house, that's nonsense. One just has to be liked, and if one is, this is about the only place where he can be in Timbuktu for months and still come staggering into the front door to be greeted with a cold drink and a friendly hand (or a Continental kiss for the ladies) as if he'd been there earlier in the day. But if one should have been there and a few hours later returns in different company, there's no "back again" greeting . . . discretion is the rule.

The truth about this great saloon is that a man can spend a couple of hundred dollars on a dinner for four, or come in to nurse one drink and chip away at bar pretzels all night, and he's welcomed either time. In fact, several creatures of habit who lean on the bar for their midday "coffee break" are known to take one or two drinks and then slip unobtrusively off to Nedick's for lunch.

The chief executive of Norton Simon, Inc., David J. Mahoney, a power risen up out of the Bronx to become one of America's most vital corporate managers, grew up at the bar of "21," where he said he made some of his most useful contacts. There, when he was short of funds, he used to "be visible for hours over one drink" in order to meet the right people. Today, with money to burn, Mahoney still prefers "21" to all other restaurants in town.

Bob, Pete, Jerry, and Sheldon

George Jessel once told a TV host-interviewer, "You can get a pretty good meal at '21' for about twenty-one thousand dollars." The next day when Jessel lunched in the club he was given a check for $21,000. Fortunately, Harpo Marx was with him and solved the problem by simply chewing and swallowing the thing. "21" has always been known to have stiff tabs, and Damon Runyon once said that the proprietors kept a secret hideaway where they crept off to laugh after presenting clients with totals. And after Groucho Marx saw the menu prices—the story goes—he ordered one bean, then sent it back to the kitchen to be peeled!

Billy Rose, known as "The Number One Buck-Preserver," once shrugged at a fifty-dollar tab for lunch with Gypsy Rose Lee, saying, "It's worth it . . . it's only half-a-point on one hundred shares of A.T.&T." Rose was then a man worth some twenty-five million dollars. Drama critic George Jean Nathan, a man known to be extremely thrifty, used to quibble over his check at the club, once questioning a three-dollar total and saying he owed only $1.95 for a pot of tea. The headwaiter stood firm on the bill until Pete stepped in and told him, "Leave it at Nathan's chintzy estimate, he's part of our floor show, he stays in the act."

A fluff-headed starlet came mincing into "21" one night, clinging tightly to the arm of an aging patron; she quickly looked around and was heard to squeak, "You call *this* something special?"

Certainly there's no snappy décor in Jack & Charlie's enjoyable mouse trap: for all its worldliness, it offers up mostly a lot of homey touches. A visiting Englishman calls it "a mélange between our pubs, provincial hotel lobbies, and an old-fashioned New York resi-

Remington bronze viewed by Pete, Mrs. Peg Coe, and publishers R. L. Jones of the Tulsa *Tribune* and James L. Knight of the Miami *Herald*.

dence." Yet it's high on pure Americana. The Cincinnati *Enquirer* once called it "a combination of early McKinley, middle Harding, and late speakeasy." As financier Michael Apostol says, "It's a clubby house. I go to certain bars where there are a lot of people I know and I feel very much at home in them, but they're not hospitable in the sense that '21' seems to be. You go through this lounge and suddenly you're protected."

The L-shaped lobby has changed little except in size from that snowy New Year's Eve of 1929 when Jack and Charlie set up their speakeasy shop at No. 21 West Fifty-second Street. To the left on entering the lobby is the coatroom, where Robert Benchley on a rainy day once directed the lobbyman, as if to an old family retainer, to "get me out of this wet coat and into a dry martini." Though one might expect to see coatroom attendants who are dignified ladies with peacock feathers in their hats, it is a surprise to find that the hat-check girls wear mini skirts, fluff up their hair, and have a lot of fun chewing gum.

Beyond the coatroom is a narrow stairway leading to the upstairs dining rooms; beyond the stairway is the door to the barroom, and across from the stairs is the tobacco counter. Here you find the books of contemporary authors such as John le Carré, Studs Terkel, Richard Condon, John Updike, and young Peter Benchley (whose father, Nathaniel, and grandfather, Robert, have had *their* days at the counter, too), often perused by some of the people who make them possible: publishing executives Nelson Doubleday, John Sargent, John Stevenson, Harry Abrams, Tom Guinzburg, Jerry Mason, Harold Steinberg, and Nat Wartels.

Next to the tobacco counter is the unmarked door to the men's room (if you have to *ask*, you don't belong). Inside the lavatory the raucous humor of the muraled walls gives some men a kick, and turns some others off. One who is definitely not still amused by

Jerry, Sheldon, Bob, and Pete, purveyors to the hungry and thirsty who have money

them is the artist himself, the painter and muralist Charles Baskerville, who maintains with some annoyance that "they were painted on canvas in my studio and shown at a private exhibition as a joke some fifty years ago. What was a joke *then* is not a joke *today.*" Otis, the deacon of the men's-room attendants, who has been with the club since 1949, is a jovial gentleman with an air reminiscent of a headwaiter on the old Lackawanna Railroad. Tips, usually fifty cents to a dollar, are thanked by "May the Good Lord be with you." If no tip, philosopher Otis has been known to say of a stingy man, "Well, he'll be taken care of."

A right turn from the front of the lobby takes the visitor to the main lounge, the unmarked door to the ladies' room, and the telephone switchboard. Around the corner is an elevator to the dining rooms upstairs, and a small "back door" into the barroom.

Few people see the front of "21" without its hustle, bustle, and commotion of people, kisses, and little exchanges of gossip and news between management and patrons. But if one can disregard the porridge of people, he will see a lobby and lounge sporting gray-green, swirly carpeting that butts up against a plaid pattern, the two totally discordant but somehow part of the sporty character of the place. Set off against the carpets are wood-paneled and green walls, leather chairs and sofas, television sets, and a fireplace where logs crackle merrily in the wintertime, over which hangs a portrait of John Carl Kriendler. In a predominant corner is a large glass case with boots and a ten-thousand-dollar silver saddle called "The Bar '21,'" once Jack's pride and joy.

The lounge also houses part of the club's art collection, which boasts twenty-six paintings and drawings and five bronzes by Frederic Remington, a holding worth close to a million dollars. Pete Kriendler is house curator and a trustee of both the Whitney Gallery of Western Art and the Buffalo Bill Associa-

tion in Cody, Wyoming. He says, "Jack and Charlie started collecting back in the twenties, and art became part and parcel of the restaurant, particularly Western art. Our Remington bronze, *The Bronco Buster*, was Teddy Roosevelt's favorite work. The two Remingtons left of the mantel, *An Ox Train in the Mountains* and *Mule Train Crossing the Sierras*, came to us from an elderly woman who frequently visited the house with her husband. One day she called to say that he had died, and she would like to come in but knew that women were not admitted alone after five o'clock, which at that time was true. I told her to come in for dinner upstairs, and she came with friends. Later she called and told me that she wanted to offer me two Remingtons at the price her husband had paid twenty-five years previously. I bought them, and after they went up on the wall she used to come in to admire them." One time a customer ran up a large debt he couldn't pay, and he suggested that the club might be interested in taking the Remington he had under his bed in lieu of payment. The club did, gladly. The Remingtons truly fit into the masculine décor of "21"; indeed, as Maria Naylor wrote in *The Connoisseur* magazine, "the club is a setting far more suitable than the antiseptic galleries of a museum."

Pete continues: "*How Order Number 6 Went Through*, or *The Vision*, a black-and-white oil on canvas, has an interesting story illustrating a tale Remington wrote with a narrator named Sundown LeFlare, a French and Indian halfbreed who worked as a free hunter and trapper, and also served the U.S. Army as an Indian scout and guide. He was given a mission by General Nelson A. Miles to take a sealed order from Fort Keough to Fort Buford, a rough trip in which LeFlare was almost overcome by cold, exhaustion, and hunger. The spirit of a beautiful Indian girl appeared before him holding a fragrant pot of food. LeFlare followed this vision, depicted in the painting, and eventually reached Fort Buford and delivered his message."

In contrast to the western art, the house hangs oils by Stephen Etnier and Georges Haquette and a "honky-tonk" piano painting by Paul Sample, as well as a mélange of illustrations, water colors, cartoons, and other works of art by such talents as Russell Patterson, Charles Dana Gibson, Bradshaw Crandall, Dean Cornwell, and Arthur William Brown. There are also gun collections, African big-game trophies, decoys, and endless bric-a-brac, all as if one big family townhouse had collected over the years the memorabilia of a troop of boys growing up to manhood—which, of course, is just what it's done.

Periodically, dedicated ladies will sit at a small table selling benefit chances to their posh captive audience, one philanthropist being Molly Berns, who has helped raise well over a million dollars for the New York Heart Association under the aegis of the Jack Kriendler–Charlie Berns Foundation. She also has been instrumental in raising a comparable sum for education, as well as local and national philanthropies.

When the lobby is awash in raffle prizes, pegboards of raffle tickets, even such awards as an automobile tire—usually left there so long each year that it seems like Kafka's starving artist—the house has a folksy atmosphere much like a little country store in the heart of Middle America.

Probably nothing speaks more of the "cult of '21'" than a little cabinet next to the tobacco counter that houses such items as ash trays, cigarette lighters, humidors, wine glasses, and "21" specialty items—all decorated with "21" or an iron gate. From London to Los Angeles, these little items appear on tables and desks, just as one sees *Gourmet* and *The New Yorker* magazines in foreign and expatriate homes.

An exchange of tales between Pete and George Romney

10

The Long
Mahogany

One of the most tempting swoops of mahogany in the world is the "21" bar, where the Big Liver League of the world bends elbows at the curved sixty-footer from opening time until the iron gate clangs shut at night. In this kaleidoscopic oasis the pressures of a plastic society are forever banished, in a blend of eighteenth-century English tavern and old frontier saloon. It has a reputation as the friendliest bar going, and it is here that big wheeler-dealers, captains of industry, and the most talkative people in the world congregate to do more major business than is probably done anywhere else—including the Westchester Golf Course. As *Forbes* magazine has noted, when business is good, the place is swarming with munching and drinking tycoons.

Salvador Dali says of "21": "Is gold . . . is gold. I go promptly at seven o'clock, and I come away with gold in my pocket, see?" He takes out a fat wallet and pats it, then drums his gold-headed cane on the floor while he hums a ditty, adjusts his bejeweled stickpin, preens his famous moustache, and, with a couple of grand flourishes of the right hand, repeats, "Gold, gold." Rumors are that Dali has received important commissions at "21," where million-dollar deals *are* made among the tables of both old-guard and newly-minted millionaires.

And the bar is also a place for hope and for psyching out business. Television producer Grant Tinker has been quoted as saying that "If you aren't lucky as I am now with my shows, you stake out your two feet of bar space, where the CBS brass hangs out, and you hardly ever leave, except to go to the bathroom. You wait for CBS executives like Bob Wood or Fred Silverman, and you ask them ridiculous questions like, 'Did the essence come through the way you wanted it?'" That's a long way from the taproom crowd of yesterday, when the very Mayfair Michael Arlen, for instance, used to hand his walking stick over the mahogany to be refueled—it had a hollow top large enough to accommodate two dry martinis—while, it is said, he danced a fiery jig on the wooden floor, singing and eating a chicken leg all the while!

Beyond the red-and-white checkered tablecloths and the pegged wood floor, the barroom has such memorabilia as a dollar bill (serial number 0000021) autographed by John B. Connally when he was Secretary of the Treasury, bronze statues of bulls and bears, a mounted bell from engine 2121 of the Pennsylvania Railroad Company, souvenirs from the fighting fronts of World War II, and horseshoes from the famous nag Nashua, winner of the Widener Handicap at Hialeah Park, Miami, in 1956. There is an endless collection of cartoons having to do with bar life by artists including Peter Arno, Whitney Darrow, Jr., and Mary Gibson, one of whose cartoons depicts a man receiving his check from the waiter and saying, "Is this for a controlling interest in the restaurant?"

The ceiling has wooden beams from which are suspended enough "toys" to drive a bunch of boys bananas. These turn out to be eclectic symbols of the people, companies, and interests that are the "faithful" of this room. Here hang miniature airplanes, the very first items to go up on the ceiling back in the early thirties when C. R. Smith of American Airlines trudged in with a model plane. Executives of other airlines quickly followed rival suit, bringing in over the years not only their little symbols but their presidents, among them Floyd Hall of Eastern, W. T. ("Bill") Seawell of Pan Am, and Eddie Carlson of United. Other passengers of this unique ceiling collection, one that would be impossible to duplicate: footballs, basketballs, and baseballs; a Yankee miniature of Bill Virdon's "21" shirt; a statue of the New York Mets' first manager, Casey Stengel; Culligan and 7-Up trucks, a Greyhound bus; a croquet mallet, oil derricks (for such oil men as Leon Hess, J. K. Jamieson, and John E. Swearingen); copper pitchers, tankards, fire extinguishers, a crocodile, cowbells, boxes of Reynolds Wrap and corn flakes; an Oscar Mayer truck with a slogan "All Meat Wieners," and monies of various sorts (economy reminders for banking clients such as Gabriel Hauge, William Renchard, and Willard C. Butcher). And the story goes that the Hormel people hang up their hams to cure them in the fine aroma of the cigar smoke found in "21." Over and around the bar one sees flags, shields, antique pistols in cases, catchers' mitts, gold replicas of horseshoes; there are street markers, and microphones which people hope do not work, and autos, autos, autos, brought in by wheel executives, whose successors are more than familiar with the "21" bar. As a reminder for those who might misbehave, there's a hangman's noose over the center of the bar. Under the bar's rail are brass spittoons for the old-timers.

Pete Kriendler tells a story about the

The "21" barroom, a grown-up fraternity room

122

model railroad train that once was there. It seems that Jackie Gleason came in one day and said, "I gotta have that model train." Pete hesitated, then said, "Okay, if you'll give us the pool cue you used in *The Hustler*." When the train man who had brought in the miniature discovered that his gift was gone, he was a bit miffed, but Gleason gave the railroad and the story exposure on a TV show and the guy was appeased, later bringing in another model for the ceiling.

Cliques tend to congregate in their traditional standing place (there are no bar stools) at the mahogany. Three such groups who call the "21" bar home are the East Enders, the Skeeters, and the Bell or Chuck Wagon bunch. The East Enders, made up of film and advertising executives and real estate men, gather beneath their club's flag with barkeeper "Lou" Rice (Luther) to serve them.

The Skeeters, who gather at the middle of the bar, grouped by sports announcer Ted Husing back in 1951, took their name from the group's interest in races out in New Jersey where it's said that the mosquitoes were

as big as horses. Served by Bru (Mysak), current "itchers" are sports commissioners, sportsmen, and their champions, who scratch one another with bar jokes, though probably none of them has seen a mosquito in years.

The noisiest bunch at the bar is the convivial Bell or Chuck Wagon Glee Club, claiming the west-end bar space just inside the entrance door, and once called by Frank Conniff "a boys' choir of lofty ambitions but rather restricted talent." (George Jean Nathan once hailed them a "must!" saying "you *must* blow the joint as soon as they start singing.") There used to be a small chuck wagon overhead, given to "21" by Joe Cowan of The New York *Journal-American*, and there is still the famous Siamese temple bell which custom demands the members ring when they want a drink, even though Henry (Zbikiewicz), *their* bartender, might be standing in front of them having just said "Hello."

The house keeps a dossier of important dates, and when a birthday celebrant dines in the clubhouse the Glee Club voices, directed by Sheldon Tannen, will burst forth with a "Happy Birthday" blast to startle the unsuspecting client, who has probably long forgotten when he was born. They present a cake with candles, courtesy of the house, and are instructed, as Mac puts it, to "throw it over your shoulder for good luck." One day Mrs. Harold Shattuck did just that, splattering the gooey thing over the wall! This surprised Mac, not because of the mess but because, it was said, "21" had used that same cake and candles for twelve years.

Sandwiched between these three luminous bar groups drink the communications men, such as publishers Peter Fleischman and Jim Shapley, and at another spot on the sixty-footer we find the horsebreeders and owners Frank and Adele Rand, Edwin Gould, J. Blan Van Urk, and their colleagues. Fighting for bar space is the younger contingent of the house, including Skip Scott, Dennis Ogden Phipps, Henry Topping, Jr., Winfield Essex III, Winston Guest, Jr., Winthrop Rockefeller, Jr., and pretty June Wells with her group of friends—yes, the female foot is also welcome at the "21" bar rail.

It's believed that a good bartender should, on seeing an approaching client, start to prepare the man's "usual." If timed properly, drink and customer should reach the bar simultaneously. When Ernest Hemingway used to appear through the bar door, a Papa *Doble* made of four ounces of light rum and a squirt of grapefruit juice and served daiquiri-style would settle into his outstretched hand. On some days, however, Papa would say, "Since I'm not drinking, I'll just have tequila." The barmen insist they could always tell which he wanted by the expression on his face.

At "21" each customer has his favorite bartender, each of whom wields the bottles a little differently—Bru's martini is not Lou's and Lou's is not Henry's. And so on down through Max (Schelle), John (Servetnik), and "Sig" (Sigmund Bank)—who mix up some three hundred thousand drinks each year for their discriminating tipplers.

Eccentric drinkers are allowed at the bar, but not over-imbibers. A Mr. Freeman from Milwaukee had the peculiar habit of coming to the bar at least ten times a day when he was in town—about once an hour—and ordering a drink, which he downed posthaste and then rushed out only to return shortly thereafter.

Frank Lyons recalls an incident that shows the bar patrol of the proprietors. Home from the Korean War on leave, Lyons met an old friend, an Air Force officer of a socially prominent family, whose father had given him a charge account at "21" on his eighteenth birthday. The two men had a joyous reunion at the "21" bar, and they got tight fairly quickly and became rather loud. First the house cut their drinks in half (the private house code for this being *leggero*, Italian for "very light"), and then they cut them off altogether. Jerry Berns finally had to ask them to leave. Frank's friend was incensed and made a speech, claiming that Frank was a returning war hero—totally untrue—and that it was unpatriotic of the house to ask them to leave. Then, in patrician high dudgeon, he said, "Very well, we'll leave. But I want you to know that I'm canceling my charge account, and furthermore, I'm canceling my father's account, too." The boys were back two days later when they had gotten over their embarrassment, to have a drink on the house and make amends.

But exceptions are exceptions. A gold "H" is set into the bar paneling near the right end, put there by bar buddies of Harold Klem, a vice president of U.S. Trucking Corporation, who dedicated it to Klem's memory with a big drinking party. Klem was supposedly America's drinking champ and was often known to polish off some fifty-five drinks in a single day. They don't make them like that any more. . . .

However, steady tipplers are not uncommon in "21," and John W. Rumsey once described the general run of people at the bar as "those well known for their support of the working man, meaning the bartenders."

Discretion has always been part of the "21" life style, where an unwritten law seems to be that spouses in flight from nagging partners are to be shielded as in a private club. One man's storming wife once discovered his hat in the coatroom and was ready to move in for the kill when the management convinced her that the club had been reserved for a private party, and she couldn't possibly go in.

And there's the legend of a well-known old gent, a Mr. Ronald, who was in the bar one night with his Swedish girl friend. Suddenly the management seemed to be encircling a party that had just come across the room—it was the fellow's wife and son, and the owners were seating them and blocking off their vision while carrying on a conversa-

tion. In a few minutes a businessman rushed up to Mr. Ronald, colliding with the wife, who was also rushing over, and the stranger grabbed the startled young Swedish girl and whisked her away, profusely thanking the old gent for having "baby sat" with his "niece" until he, her "dear Uncle," could fetch her. Dear Uncle was a captain, quickly rushed to the rescue by the owners.

On another occasion, a man was sitting with a lady friend, actually waiting for his wife. A waiter came up and said, "Mrs. Blank is downstairs, should I let her in?" To the waiter's amazement, the man said, "This time, yes." Many ex-spouses mix in peace at "21." Henry Ford once gave a party for his daughter Ann, which brought together the host's present wife, Christina, and his remarried ex, Anne. No one thought a thing of it.

The Chuck Wagon Glee Club arriving in Chicago
to exhibit their "impeccable" voices

Glee Club voices, left to right, Jim Murray, Frank Pratt, Alexis Lichine,
Bill Gargan, Charlie Renshaw, Arthur Gray, and Billy Bloomingdale

11

That's
My Table

During an age when status symbols have all but completely lost their value, and privateness is more valued than public display, it's interesting to note that none of the established territorial rights to showcase tables has been relinquished by any of "21's" famous patrons. In fact, the pecking order remains so immutable that some otherwise adult regulars of the house have been known to scream "That's *my* table" and refuse to eat if their usual space should be occupied even by friends and they are forced to move a few paces further east in the house. Horrors . . . social ostracism and paranoia. As some devotees of "21" claim, when you head *east* you are sledding toward the big iceberg, regardless of the fact that the owners stoutly maintain that "the people make the table, not the table the people. There is no such world as Siberia . . . no one section of the house is any different from any other." (Section locations

are geographically distinguishable by the original townhouse numbers of 21, 19, and 17, although until fairly recently they had more colorful terms: "front room" to "back room.") But then what else can proprietors say publicly when the bar and upstairs dining rooms seat approximately 375 people, and the house has ten thousand charge accounts and a mailing list of twenty-one thousand?

The bar is presided over by headwaiter Peter Billia and his associate, Walter Weiss, and here the most celebrated of the spirited professional folks and the informal *fahncy* young people—the bar crowd—congregate in the first section, No. 21, or the "kitchen room." This is a direct switch on other restaurants where the area around the bustling and banging chef's kingdom is Siberia for sure. Surveying this section, one finds at special tables permanently reserved for them

129

Helen Gurley Brown, right, and friends toast Jerry Berns

"21" proprietors sample a *plat du jour*, prepared by Chef Anthony Pedretti

Jerry chats with Clare Boothe Luce during her birthday party at "21"

Upstairs dining-room sections Nos. 19 and 17

131

such personalities as film mogul Otto Preminger (where he and Irving P. Lazar had their front-page battle, during which Lazar broke a glass over Preminger's bald pate).

The center section, semi-partitioned by banquettes, is a hangout for those who like to be seen, one bunch being divorcées who like to command a view on all sides of the room where there *must be* at any hour a goodly number of bachelors and a good number of men *about* to be free.

Whatever they say, Siberia *is* the easterly section, No. 17, where some house habitués would not be caught dead. Others, more ego-secure (the young contemporaries like Michael Adler, "Bunky" Hoover, and Nicholas and James Wyeth) agree with Robert Ruark, who once wrote: "I have heard that there is a tyranny of customer-location . . . front-room people, middle-room people, and back-room people. I have heard that when some customers do not come often enough to eat all they can hold for a hundred bucks, then the management becomes testy and banishes these people to the boondocks of the back room . . . of these inner politics I know nothing. My practice is merely to walk into the joint and flop into a seat. Sometimes it's in the front room, sometimes the back. I sit where there's room to sit. If there is no place to sit, I stand. Preferably at the corner of the bar."

Alan King, who takes the right corner of Siberia by preference, once shrugged and said, "I want everybody who sees me sitting here to know I'm enjoying *real* security."

But don't think the customer is always right. It is the heavy hand of management that makes the final decision. A few years ago, Billy Rose, sitting at a table in the bar, was told to hurry up and finish his meal because he had the table of George Jean Nathan, who would soon be coming in. This was a cut for Rose, but none the less he obeyed and gave up when Nathan *did* arrive.

After all, Nathan held priority because his name was on a bronze plaque above the table, near others saying "John Steinbeck, his Table," "Billy Seeman's Table," and "Benchley's Corner." It was from this same spot that Benchley once wired the mayor of Benchley, Texas: "Greetings to Benchley Texas from Benchley Robert." Interestingly, the most recent commemoration is a plaque for Richard Nixon occasioned by a visit of the President with his family.

In the middle section, on the right corner, is a plaque saying "Bogie's Corner," words so pungent one can almost see him sitting there enveloped in cigarette smoke, emitting a slight growl at people passing by, with a Ramos Gin Fizz before him. Carrying on the family patronage but in reverse social order is extrovert Lauren ("Betty") Bacall. It's said that during her stint in the Broadway production *Applause* she dined in "21" every evening, arriving promptly at 5:30 p.m., when she would sail back to the bar, sit down, order two double bourbons and a telephone, and then call up some unsuspecting friend with the command to "Get your ass over here fast before the ice melts in your drink."

One great rule of restaurateuring is to give a guy some elbow room; not so, however, in the bar, where the tables are so close one can hardly slip a check between the checkered cloths. What made this house so successful, though, is that it started out breaking the rules and has kept it up ever since. A companionable pack of people not only profits the proprietors, it also gives a room true intimacy, a casualness that people love, and an experience described by one bar addict as being rather like "getting loaded in a New York subway." There is of course the noise, which in any other place would drive people batty, but here the regulars like it—a humming security blanket controlled by a rheostat acting in direct proportion to the glasses being emptied.

The more conservative patrons of the club dine in the quieter, more spacious, upstairs dining rooms, presided over by headwaiter Joseph Mino and his associate, Ernesto ("Tino") Gavosto, where the Front Room (running the breadth of the building) and the three dining rooms left of the stairway (spreading across the back of the floor), the Tapestry, the Bottle, and the Puncheon, are decorated in a semiformal style reminiscent of an English country dining room, and feature, on the wainscoting, an antique Georgian silver collection worth some two hundred and fifty thousand dollars.

The *numero uno* tables begin with No. 115 at the top of the stairs and work their way around through the Front Room, the most obvious and viewable being the most coveted. Here obsequious service is purveyed by headwaiters, captains, sommeliers, and waiters, who, as publisher Walter Biggs says, "talk as if they have 'Locust Valley lockjaw.'" The staff, seating and serving the regulars—who include Penny Tweedy, Ginger Rogers, former Mayor Robert Wagner, and David Susskind—serves with flair and specializes in little gestures such as they did for the late Aristotle Onassis. Just seconds before his entrance, the staff would put a bowl of ice, a cold glass, some quarters of lime, tomato juice, and Stolichnaya vodka on the table—he liked to mix his own. He also liked to have waiting for him a bowl filled with little chunks of Parmesan cheese which he took with cocktails.

And what rare and exotic fare did this man choose? Not surprisingly, he was plain-palated, preferring either steak or a "21" Burger on a toasted English muffin, a side of sliced tomatoes and onions, and—always—pickles with the entrée, a Near Eastern custom. "21" frequenter Jacqueline Kennedy Onassis, who does not like the noisiness of the barroom so she always dines upstairs, chooses nonrich dishes such as broiled lamb chops or Turbot Poché au Court Bouillon with Sauce Mousseline (poached turbot served like a "dry soup"—pieces of fish in broth with carrots and onions over the top, the sauce served on the side).

Smirnoff 100-proof vodka is the drink of Joan Crawford, another regular of the upstairs, and undoubtedly one of "21's" most steadfast and devoted patrons; her usual entrée order is calves liver with bacon, and a spinach salad with lots of vinegar and lots of bacon. Producer Joe Levine comes to this room for his usual order of broiled Boston scrod; the Fisher brothers dine daily on broiled flounder; Edgar J. Kaiser on boneless baby pheasant stuffed with wild rice and *pâté*; Polly Bergen comes for the Sauce Maison. (Obviously the quirk of people who dine out regularly in the same restaurant and order the same thing is much more prevalent than one would think.)

"Whether in the bar or upstairs, we have to watch several things about seating," Mino explains. Mino, born in Italy, trained in London and at the Barclay before coming to "21" in 1946, says that "no 'ex' next to an 'ex' —we alert each to the other being in the house —and no oilman next to another; and if we see a lady in a certain Halston or Pauline Trigère gown and another coming in wearing the same design, we have to make a fast table switch. Lawrence Tibbett, a man on the tall side, insisted on not being seated next to short women."

The big problem for "21" is what to do when everyone seems to be in town and clamoring for their own tables, which obviously do rotate among certain famous figures. "Dressing up" a room, which is putting the beautiful people front forward, means finding enough showcase tables, as well as considering the size of a party and who made the reservations first (reservation slips are dated by machine when taken, a precaution against mixups and later squabbles). "These things we handle pretty well," Mino explains. "It's the unexpected—usually from the waiters—that's a little different." He smiles and recalls the day a waiter made a grand-flourish presentation of an omelette, lifted it high for the diners to see, and then released it to what he thought was a plate under his hands. The supporting waiter had failed to put down the plates, however.

A waiter once tripped and spilled a two-gallon wine bucket of ice and water over a center-table hostess in the Front Room; he paused, gasped, paled, cried, "Pardon me, Madam," and fled into the night—never returning to claim his salary or street clothes.

As is the case downstairs, the cold shoulder of the upstairs is felt in the easterly section and also in the three rooms on the north side of the floor, where the "Saturday people" —the tourists who flow in, particularly on weekends—are supposedly stashed away. "Some like the quietness," the owners say, "and the food and service are the same." (Tongue-in-cheek?) Many newcomers calmly accept Siberia—one does have to start somewhere—as do many who are truly secure, a finger-countable few. For business or pleasure, "21" is a place where people crunch in to be *seen*, not to have an intimate dinner for two, or be hidden away.

The very worst banishment of the house is to Table 34. If you're ever assigned that number, head for the woods. Getting past the Cerberus eye of the front-door receptionists is no full endorsement—you might be turned away at table, and Table 34 is code for "get him out of here." There is no such table; the number comes from the code put on the yellow card used in the speakeasy era, which meant exactly the same then as it does today: Let him sit in the lounge or stand at the bar until he gives up and goes away.

Getting a table doesn't always mean happiness. There is the story of a first-timer who ordered his dinner indiscriminately and loudly, then asked for the check and then to see one of the owners. "I've been over here in Siberia," he complained to Bob Kriendler, "I've spent over two hundred dollars for four people, and you give that guy over there [mentioning a chap by name] one of the best tables. Why, I could buy and sell him!" Bob explained, "Yes, but you can't buy what that gentleman has—a charge account with us for twenty years, plus the fact that he is a very nice man."

Helen Gurley Brown, editor of *Cosmopolitan* magazine, likes to talk about how she finally crashed the seating by simply being for months on end a constant and lavish spender . . . the house couldn't ignore her. Helen said she knew she was accepted when Jerry Berns first kissed her.

There *is* one way to get an unmitigated upper hand in this house: Book a private party in one of the three northerly rooms of

the dining floor, or in one of the upstairs rooms: the Hunt or Frontier on the second, the Jack, Winchester, or Remington rooms on the third. (Sorry, there are no private rooms for two, old Continental style; ten is the minimum.) These banquet rooms vary in décor and size from the large, trophy-filled Hunt Room to the intimate little Jack, which was Jack's drawing room–library when he lived above the shop.

In these rooms, just about anything goes, from turtleneck to T-shirt, tux, and top hat, as Mott the Hoople, a contemporary English glitter rock group, wore recently. The man paying the bill—$40 to $160 per person, inclusive of wines—can do what he bloody well pleases, and so can his guests. "21" has a highly active banquet department, accounting for some thirty per cent of the club's sales during peak seasons in the late autumn through the holidays and in the springtime.

Many long-time regulars feel that the banquet department has contributed to the changing aura of the club. The clientele is not only more homogenized by introductions through private parties, but more informal.

In 1973, Atheneum Publishers' party in the Tapestry, Bottle, and Puncheon rooms of "21"—*not* Siberia for private affairs—celebrating publication of their George and Ira Gershwin book, spotlighted not only a player piano whose keys played as if by an unexorcised Gershwin ghost the songs the brothers made famous, but also an "Upper West Side, Jewish home delicatessen buffet." This prompted *New Yorker* magazine's Geoffrey Hellman to comment to Alice Regensburg, of the Lynn Farnol Group Inc., who threw the bash for Atheneum, that "only you, Alice, could plan a party in '21' and serve sauerkraut and hot dogs."

At left, Bob, Nick Iannucci, and John Lindsay. Right, Robert Ruark: "21's a country store, trading heavily on cracker-barrel philosophy." Ruark with food editor Marilyn Kaytor, 1965

12

A Tasty
Pot of Soup

Dining at "21" has never done a food lover any harm, the club being considered one of the truly fashionable eating places in the country not only because of the fine brand of hospitality it purveys, and the comaraderie one finds there among proprietors and friends, but because the kitchen specializes in the kind of *haute* food loved by Americans. The house proudly presents clams, Dungeness crabs, oysters and smoked salmon, scallops and poached fish, turtle potage and hearty black bean soup, tender young lamb and properly aged beef, succulent, fresh vegetables in simple and beloved guises, and—would you believe—even a "21" Burger.

"21" is also famous for its wild game meat and birds—venison, saddle of antelope, mallard, partridge, pheasant, and quail, to name only a few such delicacies. One devotee of the latter is Francis T. Hunter, who likes his

quail roasted and served in the style of "the small bird on a large throne," which is quail on a V-shaped piece of toast with *pâté* on the top, and bread crumbs, red currant jelly, and bread sauce on the side.

Some connoisseurs of wild game birds like them on the very rare side, one a lady who, when she dines with her husband, orders mallard so "red" that her husband puts the menu in front of his face while she devours it with private greed and pleasure. In "21" the customer is served what he longs to have and truly enjoys, the management's philosophy being: "It is not what's good that you should like, but what *you* like that's good."

"Our clientele loves bland food, so we are careful of using herbs and spices and heavy or rich seasonings and sauces," Jerry says, "and our belief is in luxury dining, not gourmet dining. We are not consumed with sauces so rich that a man has to periodically go off to a spa to correct his *mal de foie*." Which is a good explanation for anyone who mistakenly assumes that "21" is a *grande cuisine* establishment only, the kind of place where one concentrates and contemplates the sauces in such a conscientious way that nothing else gets done. The "21" philosophy clearly begins with the belief that food should be pure and fresh and that the finest raw ingredients can speak for themselves if they are left to their own merits. There is no overcomplicated cooking, embellishments or disguising of natural flavors . . . a purist food attitude that the regulars love, and one that restaurants around the world are adopting.

The man who skillfully buys every single item of the $1,500,000 worth of food that annually comes into the house is quiet, unassuming Edward Quigley, chief steward. His choices, in conjunction with the desires of the chef, dictate the makeup of the menu—not the other way around—and if the scallops aren't to his liking, they aren't on the menu even if it says they are. Quigley is *dueño* to the house's staff of porters, main-

tenance people, and repairmen, and he roams the premises daily in his white butcher's coat, looking more like a house physician than keeper of the larder keys. Coming from the U.S. Air Force, where he was a commissary officer in Morocco, he has been with the house for ten years, following in the footsteps of Charles Sercus (who was married to Eunice Kriendler, the Kriendler boys' sister), and before that Gus Lux, one of the original employees of "21."

Quigley purchases not by the old-fashioned bid system, but from those who can supply the finest products. " '21' wants nothing but the absolute ultimate in quality, or it's 'Get that stuff out of here, you have two seconds,' " as Donald P. Bovers, of the Richard Roethel and Sons, Inc. and West Harlem Meat Co. Division, describes Quigley's purchasing style. "They're not hard to please so long as *they* like it," Bovers continues, "but they don't squeeze you so hard on a price that you try to give them a lesser quality in-

Below, Jerry supervises in the butcher shop. Right, house "doctor" Ed Quigley

stead of a top one. Importantly, they know good food and how to handle it once they get it into the house."

Purveyors supply beef that is "set," and the club "finishes off" the aging in its own aging room, wanting to be assured that the beef strips, for example, are held a full four to five weeks, at thirty-eight degrees Fahrenheit. Quigley's way to tell prime meat is that it must feel to the touch "like a woman's velvet glove if you ran your fingers gently over it." He tests everything coming into the house, sucking up colors and fragrances of

"Tastes are changing," he explains. "There's an increasing call for fish, the demand having tripled in ten years; and people ask for meat with less fat. It's the cholesterol problem." And in answer to those who have asked, yes, the pretzels, a famous touch of "21" presented in big silver bowls on the bar, *do* have less salt.

Supply sources keep changing, too, explains Quigley. "Terrapin for soup used to come into the house live from the Isle of Hope off the coast of Georgia, but the use of an insecticide there has killed off the critters,

the untreated products, poking through *arugola*, examining boxes of asparagus from Baja, feeling the soft-shell crabs from Maryland to see if they were taken from the water at the right moment, pinching tomatoes from Florida, closing his eyes in concentration and balancing a pheasant on one hand to check the weight.

so current supplies come from Long Island. And take Parmesan cheese . . . companies would rather sell it young than take the time —two to three years—to hold and age it.

"We're getting melons from Ecuador . . . it seems that for every ripe one these days, six must sometimes be cut open. Until three years ago the chickens were delivered fully feathered, really fresh things. Incidentally, the best canned tomatoes come from Israel, the best paprika from Paprikás Weiss, and the best truffles are the Urbani Italian brand. Wild rice formerly sat in the larder in big fabric bags, and when an order came to the kitchen a boy would run down with a scoop and carry some back to the chef, spilling half on the floor on the way . . . imagine what it would cost to handle it that way today. Times are changing all right."

A lion's share of the club's game, seafood, and imported delicacies (from bobwhite quail

ventures after they had shared mudholes and imaginary dinners together as Marines back in World War II.

Now an independent operation, the purchasing is controlled by Gerald M. Stein, president, who says, "I was an accountant just out of college when in 1960 I married Jerry Berns' daughter, Diane, and he asked me 'What are you going to do to support my daughter? Would you be interested in coming to work for Iron Gate?' Which I did . . . working my way up in three hard years from the warehouse to the top, despite being a son-

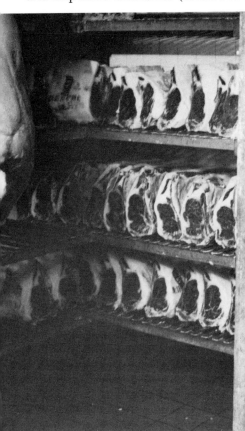
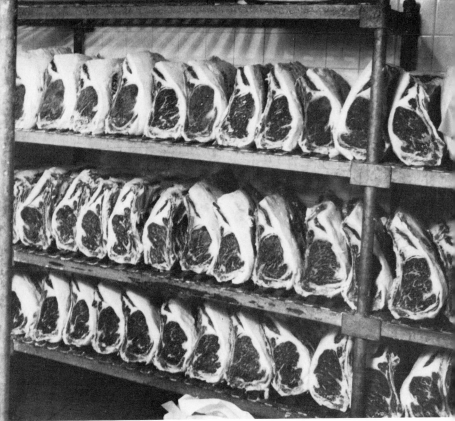

to Dover sole to frogs' legs) comes through Iron Gate Products Company, Inc. and Fidelis Trading and Fishing Company, both spawned out of "21" back in the forties. Colonel Malcolm K. Beyer (now chairman of the board, with Jerry Berns, Pete Kriendler, and Sheldon Tannen among the directors) and Bob Kriendler started these commercial

in-law of one of the principal owners. There's one thing about working for the Kriendlers and Berns, they're believers in the fact that it's just as easy to hire a relative as a stranger . . . a relative works harder, and they get you cheaper."

Of Iron Gate's annual sales of some two million dollars, about ten per cent is represented in purchases by the "21" Club, Inc., the rest internationally to major hotels, clubs, and airlines. And to fill a phone-call order for "one tin of Beluga," an Iron Gate truck will roar across Manhattan to a lady's chamber, or to an airport, to insure fast delivery to a favored customer—after all, caviar is some ninety-five dollars for fourteen ounces.

Stein travels all over the world looking for food products, buying from Scandinavia to New Zealand. Many seafood supplies come out of China. As he explains, "Game birds and meat formerly came from hunters who shot and brought them in, but the law prohibits serving wild bags; all must now come from preserves where there is Conservation Department inspection. We get beautiful mallards from the Dutchess County Rod and Gun Club Preserve. The venison comes from New Zealand, where the deer grow so

prolifically and big that they're almost a national nuisance. Sadly, Scotch grouse, once a favorite at '21,' is no longer available in its fresh form. In 1974, the law changed, and this rare little bird is only importable when cooked on the bone. That's no way to get a grouse, and there's no substitute since it must eat heather to take on that exotic Scotch grouse flavor."

Of all the Iron Gate products, none is a greater favorite with the "21" regulars than "21" Sauce Maison, that incomparable zippy red sauce, as ubiquitous at the club as Ballantine's Scotch, and used on top of "everything at the club except," as Robert La Branche once said, "the hair." This devily stuff originated back in the thirties, when Jack, Gus Lux, and Karl, a German waiter, invented it as a cure for a hangover after a challenge by Heywood Broun. Interestingly,

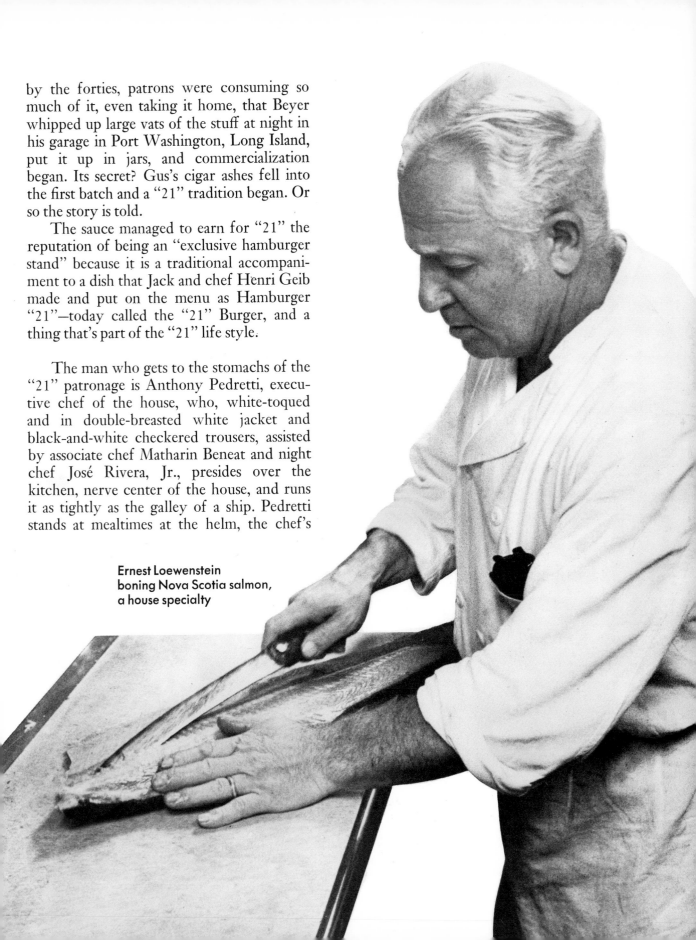

by the forties, patrons were consuming so much of it, even taking it home, that Beyer whipped up large vats of the stuff at night in his garage in Port Washington, Long Island, put it up in jars, and commercialization began. Its secret? Gus's cigar ashes fell into the first batch and a "21" tradition began. Or so the story is told.

The sauce managed to earn for "21" the reputation of being an "exclusive hamburger stand" because it is a traditional accompaniment to a dish that Jack and chef Henri Geib made and put on the menu as Hamburger "21"—today called the "21" Burger, and a thing that's part of the "21" life style.

The man who gets to the stomachs of the "21" patronage is Anthony Pedretti, executive chef of the house, who, white-toqued and in double-breasted white jacket and black-and-white checkered trousers, assisted by associate chef Matharin Beneat and night chef José Rivera, Jr., presides over the kitchen, nerve center of the house, and runs it as tightly as the galley of a ship. Pedretti stands at mealtimes at the helm, the chef's

Ernest Loewenstein
boning Nova Scotia salmon,
a house specialty

station, where for a steady two to three hours he receives orders from his captains and waiters, and scissors-sharply broadcasts them, acting as a French "*annonceur*" (announcer, or in kitchen slang, the "*aboyeur*" or "barker"), over a loudspeaker into which he pours an amalgam of English, French, Italian, and Spanish directed to the proper stations: the sauce cook, fry cook, fish cook, vegetable cook, broiler man, cold meat man, fresh fish man, and at the far end of the lineup of men in white, the salad and fruit people, and dessert and coffee experts. These specialists have their own secret recipes and methods for handling food, and they guard them well, keeping their little "black books" of culinary wisdom safely tucked away under lock and key, or under their little toques, away from the peering eyes of colleagues— and even of the proprietors, who sometimes have to literally *pry* information from their own chefs.

With a kitchen back-up force of forty-five, Chef Anthony and his cooks prepare five to six hundred meals during the short day, with the number climbing to eleven hundred during the busy autumn and pre-holiday season, and 1,250 when private parties are at their height. This number of services would drive most chefs to turn in their *gros bonnets*, but Pedretti, a trim, fast-paced, and extroverted fifty-one-year-old man with a sharp sense of humor, copes well because, he says, "I trained in hotels—the Sheraton Corporation's Sheraton-McAlpin, and prior to that the Barclay. When I came to '21' in 1959, I tell you the truth, I was used to having the hotel coffee section alone cover an area the size of this entire kitchen."

Under the guidance of Yves Louis Ploneis, the Breton chef who was successor to Henri Geib, Pedretti learned the "21" style of food and became *chef de cuisine* in 1966, when Ploneis retired. An American born of Italian parents, Pedretti had returned to Italy as a child, and was later forced into the Italian army, subsequently fleeing and eventually finding his way back to America in 1946, where he made fifty-six dollars a week at the Barclay as a fry cook. As the chef says, "That was a lot of money then." (Today, chefs' salaries start in the twenty-five-thousand-dollar area for executives, twenty thousand for associates and the chef's team.)

"My biggest problem is getting good help," Pedretti continues. "You have to train to the house . . . but today many people aren't conscientious. They don't care and have no sense of responsibility. You can't hit someone on the head to make him want to do something, you have to psychologically bring him to want to do it, if possible, and that's a very time-consuming, difficult, and expensive training chore . . . particularly, for instance, when it's a sauce chef, and he suddenly decides to leave because he can make more money as a captain or waiter, assume less responsibility, and have no heat at 'the stage' —the range." (In many restaurant kitchens, the heat can reach a sweltering one hundred and fifty degrees Fahrenheit around the stoves, but the "21" exhaust system, one of the strongest of any restaurant kitchen in town, keeps the temperature at a lower, more manageable level.)

Actually, "21" trains all of its personnel, and as Bob Kriendler once said, "We take boys who come in and show aptitude . . . they may come in as a pot walloper, and suddenly they're a vegetable man, then they seep up through the ranks. It's a real thrill when we see one of them ultimately wearing a white hat."

Two special touches of the chef permeate the "21" cuisine. The Hollandaise sauce— Pedretti makes it in two two-gallon batches about three times a day—is served on vegetables (such as asparagus, broccoli, and cauliflower) and used for miscellaneous egg dishes; extended with beaten cream and Tabasco, it becomes mousseline sauce, popularly served with poached fish—red snapper,

turbot, striped bass—and meat dishes. The other touch is the chef's liking for the perfume of "rose marie"—rosemary, which he favors over other herbs. One of the ways he employs it is on stuffed roast breast of capon, a dish that has recently become quite popular in "21," and points up again the clientele's preference for a quiet cuisine, one which is not a grand classic soup pot, perhaps, but a marvelously tasty one. This confirms a point made by none other than the late Alexandre Dumaine, sometimes called "Alexandre the Great," one of the top French chefs of the twentieth century, who, while puffing his ubiquitous Gauloise (proving that master chefs *do* smoke), was known to say, "What one can eat and digest properly at twenty-five is not the same at fifty . . . for the older person, lighter meals are preferable."

Over the past two and a half decades, the cuisine at "21" has slowly simplified from Jack's French offering to what the chef now calls "Continental American" with emphasis on such dishes as Escalope de Veau Charleroi, which is scallopini of veal with a soubise topping (purée of onions, rice, mushrooms, and rosemary essence), a coating of mousseline sauce on that, and Parmesan sprinkled over all. The dish is then set under the braizer to glaze the top.

The "21" menu, written in a combination of French and English on both the *Déjeuner* and *Diner* menus, and the Supper and Dessert cards, with miscellaneous ethnic dishes, such as *gazpacho*, listed in their original language, runs an enticing assortment of dishes and offers to a diner the chance to choose just about any kind of meal that one could want of a Continental or American mood. A *Pâté* of Chicken Livers "21," smoked trout, Wiener schnitzel, and apple pancake can give one an Austrian repast, while there are Italian choices such as minestrone, osso buco alla milanese, and Sabayon (zabaglione). Even a Chesapeake Bay buff could sort out a shore dinner from oysters, steamed clams, and crab meat, to soft-shell crabs—when they are in season, of course. In the French manner there are snails cozy and hot in rich garlic butter, steaming onion soup gratiné, leg of lamb rôti with white beans, and chocolate pot de crème. Could anyone fault a meal that began with smoked salmon and caviar, progressed on through poached fish with mousseline sauce, say an entrée of roasted saddle of lamb or venison, followed by a fragile Bibb lettuce salad, a runny-ripe Brie cheese, and a finale of garden-fresh raspberries?

Among the game meat and birds, venison chops are the top choice, an item that causes folks to flock to his house when the autumn leaves have all left the trees. Some like their chops just broiled, plain, with the venison flavor coming through loud and wild, and others prefer such flavor treatments as preiselberren sauce, a cognac-rich brown sauce set off by lingonberries, or sauce grand veneur, a tart-sweet sauce flavored with the essences of vinegar, pepper and currant jelly.

Pot pies are also popular at "21," and it's interesting to note that the top three prefer-

ences of the house's star-studded patrons come up as chicken hash, a dish that Joe DiMaggio races to the club to enjoy, the "21" Burger, and beef stew (boeuf bourguignon). In fact, any stew is popular, particularly the Irish lamb stew, a Saturday specialty. Boiled beef with horseradish sauce is a Wednesday highlight of the menu, and many regulars consider corned beef and cabbage the perfect dish to have in the tavernlike barroom.

Speaking of boiled dinners brings up New England and the fact that while the "21" menu boasts such proud desserts as Crêpes Soufflé "21" and Cherries Jubilee, the house's bread pudding, not on the menu but available to regulars, is one of the popular dessert choices.

Many "21" regulars order "off the menu," Chef Anthony explains, simply asking for a cut of beef seared bloody-rare, a grilled veal chop, or broiled turbot, plain. "People are acutely calorie-conscious," he says. "They do not want fried food, and some take salads with only lemon as a dressing. If we don't have on the menu what someone wants, we'll gladly make it for him," the chef continued.

Mrs. William Fine's favorite non-menu item is a "kind of scrambled hamburger"—chunks of ground beef in a spicy sauce. And one old-timer's love, obviously his very own concoction, is chipped beef *Véronique* (beef in cream sauce with grapes), proving the point that at "21" the customer eats what *he* thinks is good!

Charles W. ("Little Ole Baker") Lubin, the man who conceived and made "Sara Lee" into a household word, once recounted the time he asked "21" to make a particular kind of thin pancake for him. The chef whisked the batter three times before the pancakes came out perfectly, but he was as interested in the challenge as Lubin was in the pancakes.

Jerry Berns adds, "We'll make anything . . . providing it's not ridiculous or made with ingredients a kitchen would not normally store." Some regulars fall into the club in mid-afternoon to stand at the bar and "wake up" over bullshots or Bloody Marys, then they will sit down and order breakfast. Or, as one man does, ask in the late afternoon for cold roasted duck, actually a dish made for the help, who, incidentally, dine about as well as the customers. They are allowed about any food they want—within reason—and even have their own bar, including kegs of beer kept down in the scullery in the subterranean kitchen of "21."

An important point of the club's dining approach is their resolve to let a man dine in peace. A certain fine gentleman named Mr. Williams came to the club every day for lunch. He ordered luxuriously, with cocktails and hors d'oeuvre, potage, and an entrée with a bottle of wine. When he was finished, he would order another portion of the same entrée, but he never wanted a double portion to begin with, nor did he ever order both at one time. His meal continued with salad, a cheese service, dessert, and, lo and behold, a savory (always fried oysters), then coffee and cognac. After each course he fell asleep and rested precisely twenty minutes. The five-hour lunch over, he would awaken for the final time and depart. As Pete Kriendler says, "He might have been eccentric, but he

Chef Pedretti and Bob Kriendler delight in a *sauce aux morilles*, a springtime specialty

was one of the last of the people who dined luxuriously. Sadly, people don't eat that way today."

A businessman friend of the house regularly comes to the bar for lunch, sits down, and slowly drinks four whisky sours, then has six Lynnhaven oysters on the half shells, a Napoleon and coffee, savoring each sip, each bite, as if Escoffier had served up a feast.

Another belief of the house is that if two lamb chops are ordered, then two lamb chops are served, not a plate crowded with side garnishes of greens and miscellany. In "21," the money paid goes into the quality of the lamb. In fact, as Jerry explains, one of the reasons that the menu prices have held relatively firm, and not skyrocketed as other menus about town have done, is that "21" has cut down on other things besides food, and watches kitchen waste closely. As Jerry says, they are stringent about consumption of operating items, such things as electricity and water. For example, even when the club is packed, the lobby lights are not always fully turned on. Jerry, a man with an IBM-machine mind who follows the business balance-wheel nature of his brother Charlie, is often seen spinning around in a corridor to snap at a light switch like a piranha at prey. "You didn't turn out the light in the ladies' room," he'll thrust at a secretary. "You want to go back to South America?" he'll say to a Spanish-speaking boy who is peeling a potato, potato and all.

The service is normally attentive in "21," the staff moving about the dining rooms with hawk-eyed enthusiasm and concern for the needs of the diners; however, we all know that with the slow passing of the old-guard staff you *do* experience the occasional knife that comes sailing dangerously close, the wine glass with a fractured leg, the wine waiter who forgets to pour—but scowls if you remember. Some will complain that the shad roe, for instance, can be broiled to the point of rigor mortis, or the salad smothered.

Such things can happen. But as in any good house, if a mishap occurs, you should politely ask that it be corrected, not keep quiet and grumble later. "21" is one of the few places left where an honest opinion can be expressed and you do not go away with cream pie in your face.

What does it really cost to dine in "21"? As Jack and Charlie once said, "We do not charge high prices to rob people, but to keep the heels out of the joint." And as one old-timer sums it up, "'21' is a place where you can't get anything for less than twenty-one dollars! The menu is all à la carte. A bill for two for lunch, with each having a cocktail, entrée (luncheon entrées average nine dollars), and coffee, and a bottle of modest wine, would be about fifty dollars including the couvert and tip. Dinner for two, with average-priced orders, each having a cocktail, soup, entrée (dinner entrées begin at ten dollars), salad, and coffee, with a bottle of wine, will come to between seventy-five and eighty dollars including the couvert and tip. A stint at the bar and a reach for pleasure beyond *vin* pretty *ordinaire* and you must be prepared to pay. However, the same tabs may be found at other recognized restaurants about town.

Many regulars of the house never bother to sign their checks but just walk out and leave the house to tote them up and add them to their individual charge accounts. In this event, a standard twenty-per-cent tip is added to the check, plus a one-dollar minimum to the sommelier for each bottle uncorked.

When Mrs. Mary Roebling, chairman of the board of the National State Bank, formerly the Trenton Trust Company, takes her industrialist clients to "21," the bill is never presented but just mailed to her office. Anne Baxter once brought her parents to the club and, not wishing to jockey with her father for the tab—the problem all daughters have with their daddies—requested that it not be

Studying the menu for a private party

presented, but mailed to her New York residence.

Headwaiter Mino tells of a person who recently was so pleased with the service of the dining room that, when presented with a check for $132 for four people, he matched that amount with a tip of the same amount. Until the early seventies, "21" took no credit cards, accepting only house charges and that old-fashioned stuff, money.

The subject of cash, incidentally, brings up a tale. One day practical joker Sheldon Tannen was confronted by a young Texan who had never been in the club before but wanted to pay his check by signing. The man showed pocketsful of references and credit cards, but since they were not at that time accepted, Sheldon told the man "No." Ruffled, the man paid in cash, and left. Sheldon later heard through the "21" underground news system that the man had gone to a bank and applied to the Federal Reserve Board for a ten-thousand-dollar bill, and intended coming back to dine, at which time he would call for his tab and present the big bill. Sheldon arranged to handle the change with silver dollars—bags and bags—placed on a silver tray on a serving cart. When the man *did* come in and asked for his tally, the cart sallied forth. The man obviously had no sense of humor, for he simply lugged away his bags of change and never came back to the club.

13

Oh to Be Trapped in the Claret Cellar

The hearty knife, fork, and glass work at "21" includes a heavy pouring from the wine cellar, its fame once noted by Steve Hannagan, who said, "Any Turkish-bath attendant in mid-New York will attest to the fine steam aroma of '21's' wines and brandies. They say it is a pleasure to dry out a '21' man!"

Unchanged since Prohibition days, the labyrinth of bin rooms extending underneath the public floors of "21"—a sight happily shown off to visitors by cellar attendant Michael Canales—houses a veritable museum of wine artifacts, including whisky bottles from the dry days, and one of the town's—and possibly the country's—finest collections of wines. Here rests an incredible count of some six hundred and fifty different kinds including bottlings of *grand cru* Bordeaux and Domaine Burgundies, from single bottles and magnums up to Nebuchadnezzars of reds,

whites, and champagnes, and a mighty friendly group of *vins* from other countries around the world, running the gamut from California Pinot Chardonnay to Italian Barolo. This is a collection that can drive a wine lover not only half crazy at the viewing but also into fits of indecision when confronted with a choice—assuming that money is no object, of course. According to legend, a connoisseur was once trapped in the claret cellar section after a bin-room door lock failed, and was offered his choice of wine until a locksmith could be summoned. He was so distraught at the incredible choice of rare vintages that when the door was finally unlocked, he hadn't yet made up his mind what to select.

Oh, to have had his dilemma, particularly since the cellar contains museum bottlings of clarets that date back to 1865, 1870, and 1890. As T. Mario Ricci, chief sommelier, reports, "Last year I opened seven bottles of Château-Lafite 1870 . . . five were so exquisite it made one tremble to taste the wine, one was so-so, and only one was bad. For service of any wine before 1900," he explains, "we wait until the diners sit down at the table, we then uncork the wine, decant, and serve it . . . a very old wine is very fragile."

Big, beautiful, and as tempting to read as a salacious book, the "21" wine list is a most impressive tome. Bill Doerfler, who designed and printed the list in its first edition back in 1936, says, "Today's list is easier to do, simply because of the way we printed the first one, which took considerable patience. Jack was no easy man to work with, and he was so fearful of my making an error that he made me personally taste each wine and record the label of every bottle in the cellar . . . It took three hours a day for two years, opening, testing, and recording. A pleasurable job? . . . Agony! You see, in true wine-taster fashion, I had to spit the precious stuff into a bucket of sawdust. Jack wouldn't let me swallow a drop!"

Though the capacity of the cellar is between two thousand and twenty-five hundred cases, the house considers this their short-term storage, where the reds are brought up to 68–70 degrees Fahrenheit, the white held at 48. As this supply is depleted, it is replenished from a huge cache stored in a long-

term warehouse on the west side of town, where eight thousand to ten thousand cases are held at 56 degrees, among them a highly valuable collection of '61s. The total worth of "21's" cellars is enormous, even at cost.

Just like all the comforts of home, the cellars of "21" also house little private stashes for clients who have preferences for particular vintages—they pay the price of the wine at the time that it is laid away. A. B. Lawrence and Thomas Lenk of New Jersey have their private stores of Dom Pérignon and Château Margaux 1947. Lyndon Johnson's granddaughter Miss Lucinda Robb has a bot-

Below, a niche of the "21" bin rooms.
Right, Quigley and Jerry enter the wine cellar

tle designated for her twenty-first birthday, representing the "21" tradition of laying down a bottle for a newborn's coming-of-age time. Anne Roosevelt put aside a bottle for David Roosevelt Luke to be uncorked in 1990, and August Busch IV has a bottle of Ezra Brooks bourbon for *his* twenty-first, 1985, put away by Robert Charles Gadsby of St. Louis. Topping those, baby Wendy Ford, daughter of Detroiters Mr. and Mrs. Walter B. Ford III, has a bottle of brandy reserved for her by her godfather, Emory M. Ford, Jr., the grand opening date to be 1994. Other Detroiters with private stocks include Dollie and Ed Cole, Florence and "Bunky" Knudsen, Beth and James Gilmore, the Lester Ruwes, and the Edward Slotkins. Others particular of their vintages are Orin Atkins,

Herbert Allen, Gavin K. MacBain, John and Henry Ringling North, James Knott, Roy Larsen, Walter Thayer, and Fred Sullivan.

Most regulars of the house have a pretty definite idea of the wines they prefer to order, but many leave the choice to Mario (or to his associates John in the dining room, Tom in the bar, or Octavio, roving newcomer to the house sommelier fold), who explains that no one should hesitate to ask advice of the sommelier.

Many valuable vintages pass through the glasses at the club, such as Lafite 1961 for some one hundred dollars a bottle, and Margaux 1955 for about seventy-five (go ahead and weep when comparing prices to a couple of decades ago, when you would have been pressed to pay fifteen dollars for either wine of a comparable vintage), but there is a trend, as Mario says, for people to order simple wines. A savvy drinker can find good bargains in the twelve-to-sixteen-dollar category—Beaujolais and Pouilly-Fumé, and American and Italian wines—with the average order of the ten to fifteen cases uncorked daily going for between fourteen and twenty-five dollars a bottle.

In the earlier years of the club, handsome Mac, carnation in his buttonhole and fine Cuban cigar smoke trailing behind his tweeds, sailed off to France to trudge through the vineyards of Bordeaux and in countless damp cellars dip into barrels of lush Latours, Ausones, and Lafites, purchasing directly in that manner. But today this romantic type of taste-traveling is outmoded, according to Jerry: "We have about a dozen individuals concerned with the wine companies, each with a specialization, who annually submit their products to myself and Mario—we both pass judgment—and we buy directly from them, provided they continually handle the same vintners. We try to keep the same wines in the house, vintage to vintage, though we are certainly open to testing new wines of worth, from any wine-growing

Left, sommelier Mario Ricci with private reserves. Above, Mario receiving a
medallion of honor from the National Committee of the Wines of France

region or country."

"21" clients are equally open to trying new and different drinks. Robert Gourdin, a national sales manager with Schieffelin & Company, remembers an interesting incident from the time when he was a sommelier at "21" back in the fifties and sixties, and, at twenty-four and looking very cherubic, was the pet wine man of such notables as Rex Harrison, Danny Kaye, Prince Bernhardt of Holland, Ronald Reagan, and Greer Garson. It seems that *the* Mr. Astor came into the

him, Mr. Astor asked for a carafe, and told Robert to make a "sangría." Robert was torn between following the man's request, since the management's policy is that the customer is always right, and *not* mixing up all those good things to a terrible fate, but "I turned my head and stirred up the expensive concoction, which came in the end close to fifty dollars." And how many drank it? "Only Mr. Astor," recalls Robert.

Left, connoisseur Mac holds a wine-tasting.
Below, Mario with rare old ryes and bourbons

club one day and asked to have a bottle of La Tache Monopole, Domaine de la Romanée-Conti 1947 (then about thirteen dollars), a bottle of Dom Pérignon 1947 (about fifteen dollars), an order of cognac and Curaçao, followed by orders for plates of fresh cucumber rind, strawberries, raspberries, blueberries, and pineapple. When all this was before

A man who knows his wine is Baron Enrique DiPortanova, of Houston, who comes in with friends such as Mr. and Mrs. Stass Reed and Princess Obolensky and has fine wines and very elaborate lunches, which start at about 2:00 p.m. and, as management says, "end when we sweep them out." A typical lunch for eight people brings the tab to twelve hundred dollars, though this includes expensive cigars, the house reports. At one hundred and fifty dollars per luncher, indeed there *would* be a little something left for cigars, and a little for the service people. But as one person commented, "What would one do for supper, and a postprandial drink?"

Interestingly, among the after-dinner drink choices, port seems to be gaining favor with "21" regulars, who have usually been dedicated brandy drinkers addicted to armagnac and cognac. Some today are also sipping into Carlos Primero, a fine Spanish brandy. The once-famous liquor cart which was wheeled around to diners, offering a choice of some two dozen after-dinner soothers from Grand Marnier to Strega, seems to have lost favor. "That's possibly because the taste of our patrons is becoming drier," explains Mario.

Speaking of cigars reminds one of Oscar Wilde, who said of tobacco that, like himself, it is a perfect pleasure: it is exquisite and it leaves one unsatisfied.

"21-ers," ladies included, puff away a tremendous number of fine cigars, enough to make snappy annual sales of close to a million dollars in tobaccos and related smoking accessories for "21" Club Selected Items, another company birthed out of the club. This big little venture, with Sheldon Tannen as president, got started back in 1959, when Sheldon, who had learned about cigars from Mac, a connoisseur who foresaw the need to do something about "21's" cigar supply, then under private Cuban label but threatened by the political climate on that island.

With the Castro takeover, the U.S. Government banned the importation of Cuban tobacco leaf, and smokers were left high and dry with two fingers raised in the air as an empty victory sign. Fortunately, Mac and Sheldon, creative guys that they were, had jumped onto a plane and gone to Cuba's Pinar del Rio, the famous tobacco province, and

bought up, just before the embargo, about a million cigars for $250,000. When they arrived in New York, a special humidor warehouse was built with a steady sixty-percent humidity where the cigars were given a comfy house (good cigars, like good wine, can actually mellow and improve with aging).

The "21" boys waited, and when Cuban leaf prices shot skyward, the stash of pre-Castro cigars started a new business for them. Friends of "21" bought up vast quantities to hoard away for personal use, and other restaurants and hotels came calling to see if they could buy some of the "21" supply. The club cooperated, and stepped into the cigar business.

In the interim, Sheldon had sewn up the considerable talents of the best U.S. hand-rolled cigar company, the Gradiaz-Annis Company (now a division of General Cigar Company, Inc.), in Tampa, Florida, who guaranteed Sheldon all their cigars made of

Cuban leaf for as long as their supply lasted. When *that* gave out, the company started rolling blends of Nigerian, Sumatran, Ceylonese, Brazilian, and Colombian leaves, which were the best to be had though not the equal of fine old Cuban products. Today, Cuban-seed tobacco is being grown in Nicaragua's Esteli region and is coming up as a strong supply for cigar rollers in Miami, the center of the handmade-cigar industry, where Cuban refugees hand-roll some thirty million cigars a year. But Gradiaz-Annis still makes its own, supplying "21" with private-label smokes in many shapes and four color classifications: *natural* (light), *colorado* (copper-colored), *claro* (greenish), and *maduro* (dark). Though the club carries non-private labels, including fine Canary Island cigars, whose quality became recognized here during the sixties, the home products are offered first when clients ask for cigars.

As to the cost of "21's" cigars, George Jessel once stopped at the tobacco counter and bought three cigars, giving in payment his endorsed check from ASCAP for six-months' royalties on his song "My Mother's Eyes." The clerk obligingly accepted it and then said, "Mr. Jessel, sir, you're forty-two cents shy."

There's also the story of the time when Robert F. Wagner was mayor and took some principals and mediators of a threatened municipal strike to dinner at "21." When all had dined and wished to talk, not over a peace pipe but good cigars, Wagner asked for the private stock of Ambassador Norman K. Winston, his good friend and official municipal greeter. Everyone puffed and talked for three nights in "21," and the threatened strike was settled just as Mr. Winston's supply gave out.

Cigar-puffer and jewelry designer Maggie Hayes, left. Below, Bob with Mayor Robert F. Wagner, Jr., left, and brother-in-law the late Kenneth Steinreich

14

We Have Tried
Nepotism and It Works,
Hurray

If the hospitality that a restaurant purveys depends in large part upon the ratio of employees to patrons, then "21" should be considered a perfect host. The house's seating capacity of 450 is staffed by a minimum of 250 people, with the number swelling to 280 during the busy seasons. This big family of employees means an annual payroll of over $2,500,000 not including Social Security and other benefits.

The club has a profit-sharing plan for non-union people, and medical and pension benefits too. The computer system used for recordation, billing, and salary payments keeps tabs on any money lent to employees, and held for them, and the house also takes out for government bonds, and acts as adviser to their people, most of whom, it's jokingly said, leave the club feet first. Over half of the employees have called "21" home for all of their working lives, and there is a "21-

Year Club" with fifty-five members, half of whom have been in the house over thirty years. Moonlighting is not discouraged, so long as an employee gets enough shuteye to perform during working hours. Fred Porcelli, host in the bar, has acted as a maître d' in CBS soap operas, and bartender Bru has been seen on Western TV shows.

For those exposed to the greasing of the palm (and in "21" that can mean about anyone), tips are understandably generous. No one will ever know, except *maybe* the Internal Revenue Service, just what tips some of the employees do make, but it is said that they do quite well. Old-timer bartender Emil used to collect apartment buildings, and the captains and headwaiters speak casually of their "vacation homes." At holiday times, when patrons are sentimentally generous to their friends who man the house, keeping the whisky flowing and the plates hot, the tips

164

are said to be amazingly high.

Waiters, busboys, and bread boys share in the standard fifteen-per-cent tip, a captain receives the standard five per cent, and a headwaiter's gratuities are usually a dollar or more for guiding a party to its table. Sommeliers are tipped a minimum of a dollar per corked bottle, some uncorking as many as forty-five bottles a day. Part of "21's" successful formula is superb service. There are enough people wandering around the club to take care of *anything*, and a diner can hardly think about picking up a cigarette without having a lighted match immediately hit its tip. It's certainly not the place to stop smoking, or object to being pampered.

But the loyal staff hasn't always been on hand. In November 1972, during a strike of cooks, waiters, and bartenders, "hungry and thirsty patrons flocked in and there we stood," Sheldon recalls. "It looked chaotic and hopeless." But in the "21" spirit of camaraderie, such beautiful patrons as Liz Whitney pitched in to help, donning aprons along with immediate members of the Kriendler and Berns clans and friends—about a dozen people to replace some one hundred and thirty employees.

This gang flipped the aura of dignified "21" back to the informal tone that had prevailed there during the thirties and forties when swashbuckling and Scotch-drinking writers were known to grab white coats and go into the kitchen to cook or to play waiter. Writer and producer Arthur Kober, playing bartender, supposedly once threw eggs across the bar because there was a director of two-reelers in the house.

It was during the strike that the Chicago Tribune carried on its front page the headline: *Onassis Has Knockwurst at '21,'* as indeed he did, and a ten-dollar one, coming in and saying "What am I going to have, Bob?" to which Bob Kriendler, a chap who had a whimsical reply always ready, said, "Well, we have hamburgers and we also have

'kosher hot dogs,'" and he showed a plate on which rested a half-eaten wurst and held it close to Onassis's nose. Onassis ordered not only the wurst, but also a vodka on the rocks, mustard, and a bottle of beer.

John Edelstein, a junior executive with W. R. Grace & Co., moonlighted as a "sous chef" in "21" during the strike, and as he recalls: "I raced from my day job to get to my new night job, called in by Jeff Kriendler, Bob's son, who also gathered together other friends of ours from Deerfield including Tim-

"21" proprietors turn chefs to replace a striking kitchen staff

othy Racine and Tom Coopat, who worked on the floor, and Doug de Marco and Johnny Bendel, who helped tend bar. Florence Kriendler, Bob's wife, and Martha Berns, Jerry's wife, and Cecily Berns Miller, their daughter, and Sheldon's wife Ellen, helped Jeff and me man the battery of stoves under the direction of management associate Terry Dinan—a wizard with food. Would you believe that we actually turned out the nightly dinner orders, even catering a party of two hundred who knew and accepted our amateur status?" Molly Berns supervised the bar dining area, where Ann Dinan, Marcia Snyder, and regular customer Ben Givandan waited on table.

John had never really cooked before, but as he said, "For some reason they thought I had, so I didn't say anything because I thought it would be fun. We made simple hors d'oeuvre—fresh shrimp, herring, crab meat, prosciutto, and things we just arranged on service plates. The entrées were limited to duckling and filet, and the rest of the menu was asparagus with Hollandaise and a dessert of strawberries in liqueur. I learned that really great raw food carries itself; we didn't have to hokey it up. I was amazed . . . those pots and pans, even empty, weigh a ton. We didn't finish washing them or the dishes until the sun came up."

Patrons pitching in to help the house in time of trouble is a suitable reciprocity to the considerations the club has long bestowed upon its clientele. As extroverted and people-minded Pete, the catalyst of the house of "21," says, "We still cash checks and advance money to regulars who forget to do their banking, and our receptionists perform all kinds of miracles for clients, such as getting impossible theater and airline tickets, calling limousines, reserving tables at night clubs, and in general offering the services of a good concierge in a European hotel."

Thousands of dollars are poured each year into baby gifts—each pet patron's new

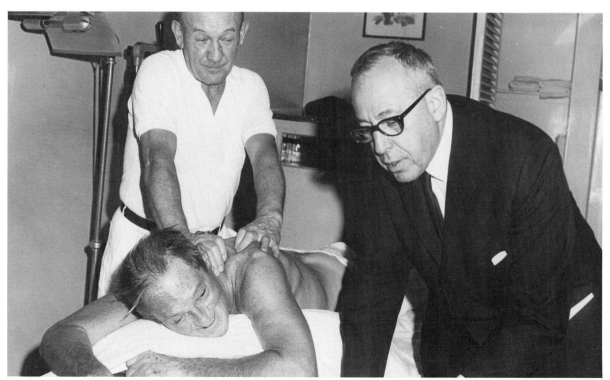

Above, Sven Erickson massages Pete, who privately confers with Jerry. Right, upstairs in Pete's office

arrival receives his personal recognition—and humidors and Christmas gifts to favorite patrons, including cuff links for men and silk scarves for ladies. Which brings up a little tale as told by photographer Barrett Gallagher. It seems that a friend of his, Howard Reilly, director of the Fred Allen radio show, invited Gallagher to watch a program from the control booth. Since he and his wife, Timmie, had met Reilly through "21," they wore their many Christmas scarves from over the years draped on every available limb. Getting to the show, they met up with Minerva Pious and Henry Morgan, who looked up and said, "I see you're familiar with '21.'" To which Minerva quickly responded, "Familiar with it? They get all their clothes there!"

For many years, traveling authors, writers, newspapermen, husbands in hiding, and busy executives have used the "21" switchboard as their personal telephone service. Frank Buck, for example, after some months off in the wilds of Borneo, would walk in and extend his hand for messages. The extent of this service is often a bit extreme; as operator Doris McAleer says, "We've never been able to figure out why patrons call us for the telephone numbers of hotels and friends instead of calling information!"

"21's" table phone service is as famous as the club, and when a call comes in for someone, pageboy Julio prances through the house holding up a slate with the recipient's name. This service isn't totally gratis, however; there is a charge from both the table and the switchboard phone booth. After all, the people at "21" can afford it. As one friend of the house said, "When you see a guy phoning and talking and gesturing and eating all at the same time, he's got to be somebody important." Actually, many status seekers who dine here bolster their egos by having their friends or office call them—the show's the thing at "21."

The habit of planting carnations on the

lapels of favored male customers—a symbol of the club and a thirty-dozen-a-day-gesture that blooms all over the house—provoked Chicagoan Ben Hecht to once write:

We came to town in chicken crates,
Threadbare and daft from wind and sun.
Don Quixotes from the prairie states,
Lumberjack poets from Oregon.
Weep not, oh muses, be still. Art rates
A red carnation at "21" . . .

A friend who falls on rough times will still be welcomed into the club, following the policy that Jack and Charlie set in Depression days. Frank Lyons recalls the story of a "21" regular who happened to have signed notes which put him in a difficult financial situation, so he had to cut down, a pinch here and there, one thing being his some two-thousand-dollar-a-month spending at the club. When he hadn't shown up there for several weeks, Jerry Berns called him, saying, "George, we've missed you, we hope you haven't been ill or anything?" George explained his situation; "I just can't charge." Jerry said, "Nonsense, you've been a great customer for many years. Come in any time you want, and when you're ready pay us back." The man did, and after correcting his problem, he became an even bigger spender in the club, which had carried him for one full year.

Author Edward Keyes tells a story of the time he was in his "lowers," waiting for a big royalty payment from the film rights to *The French Connection*, made from the book on which he had collaborated, and unable at the moment to pay his bar bill at "21." The club sent him the usual letter, and then Jerry started calling him at night and on weekends. "I was embarrassed," Ed says, "but it's a restaurant I respect and I want to be regarded there with at least minor affection. My wife, Eileen, finally explained the situation and Jerry said, 'Gee, that's all right, if you'd told me in the first place I wouldn't have bothered you,' even corroborating it by letter. What a classy way of handling it. Naturally I paid the bill when I could."

On the other hand, Ludwig Bemelmans once said, in writing to Leonard Lyons about his love affair with New York, "I would like to be buried in '21's' cellar, with the Kriendlers standing by in dark suits, each holding a burning candle in one hand and in the other my large unpaid bills."

Ward Morehouse once wrote of Jack Kriendler's money-lending policy: "I stood at the four-deep bar and told Jack that I'd like

to talk to him when he got a minute. He gave me a quick look and said, 'What's the matter?' 'Nothing much,' I said. 'I want to borrow five hundred dollars—right now.' Jack looked at me steadily for an instant, smiled, and said, 'See you a little later.' He then took command of the bar traffic. Within five minutes he was beside me and handed me five hundred dollars in currency.

" 'Glad to let you have it,' he said. 'I just want to say one thing: pay me back. I don't want to lose a friend.'

Until the sixties, the club offered a very élite little barber shop and gym service on the third floor. If a man came in feeling a little rumpled or pecky, or maybe needed to shape up before going home to his wife, he could get straightened out under the watchful eye of John Sideri, once Mark Hellinger's personal barber, who presided over the steam cabinets, weights, medicine ball, jumping rope, massage, and valet services—facilities still in the house and available to close friends of the owners.

Once Robert Ruark almost burned up under the sun lamp . . . probably coming to at just the right moment and muttering, "I'm daid," a favorite expression of his, his last words when he went to sleep and the first when he woke up. He was the maker and brunt of many a joke around his favorite bar. In *The Iron Gate of Jack & Charlie's "21,"* a second edition published in 1950 to commemorate the twenty-fifth anniversary of "21," John Crosby fantasized living in the root cellar of "21" with a bag of truffles as a pillow, and only an occasional guest: "Apart from the trolls, I'm left alone when the place shuts up for the night except . . . one night I stumbled over Robert Ruark in the alcove of the lower dining room. At first blush, he appeared asleep. He wasn't, though. He was dead. The next morning, the porter slipped a few mouthfuls of Mac's 1812 brandy into him, there was a brisk billow of flame from his lips, and he sat up and yawned. . . . Where other people fall asleep, Ruark expires. . . . He says he gets more rest dead than otherwise."

It was Sir Cedric Hardwicke who, after having a "once over clean" and all the complete services of the salon, facetiously said, "A man can spend his entire life inside these walls enjoyably—except to leave now and then to eat."

Speaking of food, one of the club's special services once was to supply boeuf bourguignon, steak tartare, or filet mignon to pooches, who were welcomed into the club until some silly law said they had to stay home. Canines called such names as Little Níspero Randel, Popo, and Eury were among the lounge loafers along with the famous such as Lucius Beebe's St. Bernard and Dali's ocelot (*all* pets were welcome) who were tethered to little gold rings on the baseboards in the lounge. Unfortunately, a couple of little old ladies, each with about twenty million, came in one day, leashed up their friends, filled up on martinis, and then made off with the gold rings when they left. (The management simply put the charge on their ticks, standard practice in a case like this.) Brass rings, larger and less desirable, were installed, and some of them are still in the lounge waiting for the law to change.

Julius Hallheimer's wire-haired dachshund, Schmoolie Boy, was the only pet allowed free run of the lobby. Late at night he'd go to the barroom door—never farther —catch his master's eye, and stand there staring until he was taken home.

Another story goes that one day a gorgeous bachelor lady's poodle suddenly wrestled from her arms and raced to throw himself, whining and crying in joyous ecstasy and personal greeting, upon a gentleman who had just come in with his wife. The man didn't try to explain that one.

But canine catering "21"-style has not totally ended. Recently, "21" made a birth-

The daily luncheon-tasting in the barroom

day cake for one of the classier pooches about town, a culinary triumph featuring chopped meat and brightly trimmed with rosettes made from carrot, parsley, and potato purées. "What will we charge for it?" Chef Pedretti asked Pete Kriendler, who replied, "Oh, five hundred dollars." Then he paused and said, "Well, better make it sixty."

"Don't you ever get tired of each other?" one might ask a band of impeccably tailored

Berns, sixty-eight, vice-president and secretary; Sheldon Jay Tannen, fifty, vice-president and treasurer. In the early seventies, two young restaurant men, Terrance ("Terry") Dinan, thirty-one, and Bruce W. Snyder, thirty-six, joined the "21" management team (Terry having come up through the kitchen), and they now form part of the daily family meetings. Though neither of the boys is related to the owners, it's interesting to note the clannish resemblance they're taking

Bob receives honor from Italian Ambassador Egidio Ortona, 1971

noshers who twice daily, at 11:30 a.m. and 5:30 p.m., gather at a table in the entrance room of the bar—a banquette for lunch, a center one for dinner—and vibrantly exchange gossip, welcome guests into the club, make and take phone calls, and gesture while they taste specialties of the day and eat "off the menu" in such an interesting manner that regulars often check what they're eating before ordering themselves.

They are, of course, the cousins—lock, stock, and barrel owners of "21": H. Peter Kriendler, seventy, president; H. Jerome

on. And last year, in 1974, to the delight of the "21" patrons, Charlie Berns's son, Anthony ("Tony") David Berns, thirty-five, a Cornell food man, came into the business after having been out on his own for some ten years to gain wide managerial experience.

Work is this executive staff's passion, and possibly its anodyne. The men set the style and pace of busy, bustling "21," hire the staff, check the carnations, poke into the pretzels, and test the salt shakers to make sure they run freely, as well as personally greet each guest, and take care of such client eccentricities as baking a hundred-thousand-dollar diamond engagement ring in the soufflé for a young lovely at her soon-to-be fiancé's request. These men rarely pause during their day except to take a brief siesta and massage and change their custom-made clothes, a habit performed frequently upstairs. In fact, true to the tradition of Jack and his Mr. Spitz, Mr. Joseph, the house tailor, follows the boys about the club holding out buttons and fabric for the busy men to consider.

trigued that they have made the restaurant and bar business *big* business, one where a large family can perform for one common and profitable cause; one that has taken these men far, making them wealthy to lengths that some of their customers can only aspire to. (As an interesting aside on their similar tastes, the favorite off-hours fun of these gurus of the restaurant business is to sneak off to a favorite Chinese restaurant.)

This all-in-the-family operation, called by

Pete and Jeanette Kriendler

Being in the restaurant business means experiencing one of the longest, hardest, most grueling of days. Not only do the men work in their offices in the mornings, but they are also on the floor while the club is open—from 12:00 noon until about 1:30 a.m., six days a week, except during the summer when the boys take Saturdays off, spend their weekends out in the Kriendler-Berns compound in Westhampton Beach.

Looking closely at these successful men, their awareness of what they have achieved, and their extraordinary unity, one is in-

Pete "nepotism that works," in which each member has an office on the floors above the club, and each is a contributor to the profitable operation of the organization, helps keep alive the mystique that is the most valued asset of "21."

Missing from this contemporary team is I. Robert Kriendler, whose two-decade reign as president of the club ended on August 15, 1974. Bob had been away from the restaurant from April until August, recuperating from open-heart surgery, and after only one week back at the club, where he presided again over his weekly staff meetings and purveyed that special VIP treatment to guests, he died suddenly at his summer home at Westhampton, leaving the heritage of "21," his second home, to be guarded by brother Pete, Jerry, and Sheldon, and their associates, Bruce, Terry, and Tony.

Sixty-year-old Bob held, at his death, the rank of colonel in the Marine Corps Reserve as a retiree. Colonel Alexander W. Gentleman, U.S.M.C., Retired, Bob's closest friend since they met on Guam during World War II, called him a man "with a gift for friendship." On his death Louis Sobol made the comment: "It is rather too early a passing of a man who was part of an era."

It was at "21" one night that Jack Warner first thought of selling the Warner Bros. studio. Asked to name his price, he said, "Since we're at '21,' let's make it twenty-one million dollars." No sale was made, and he finally sold it for thirty-two million. It's said that both Warner and Goldwyn, men who led industries rampant with nepotism, regarded the "21" operation as among the most successful examples of "family favoritism" since Orville and Wilbur Wright.

Many people have tried in vain to buy this famous house on West Fifty-second Street. Almost successful was the development subsidiary of the Ogden Corporation, whose president, architect, and entrepreneur, Charles Luckman, got as far as the paperwork in the purchase of the club back in 1969, the terms being that the "family" would stay on and run things the way they always have;

Right, they run "21": Pete and
Sheldon, foreground; Tony and Jerry, center;
and Bruce and Terry

Pete and Sheldon with the Renshaw sisters

there was to be an exchange of stock worth well over $12,500,000 for acquisition of the club, which then grossed about $4,500,000, and its two subsidiaries, each grossing about $2,250,000, all physical assets including the art work and silver, and the building itself, valued at about $3,000,000. The owners were prompted to this move in an attempt to secure their estates, but the deal didn't cover a drop in the market. When it dropped, the Wall Street recession lowered the value of Ogden stock, and the deal fell through—much to the relief of "21" patrons who were not happy with the thought of the club relinquishing any control to "outsiders."

Will the owners sell "21?" "Yes, you can have it for twenty-one million, the folding green paper kind," Jerry says, adding that "No matter what happens to the corporate structure, the intent is to run a 'family business.' Whenever we have been approached by another entity, on a merger or takeover, usually the first clause presented to us is that the family force must stay on. There must be continuity, we must keep the '21' tradition alive."

When asked what younger members of the family might step in, Berns explained, "There are Bob's two sons—John Carl ('Jack') and Jeffrey—and there is Sheldon's son Richard. Both Jeffrey and Richard are professionally schooled in the restaurant and food business. In the Berns clan, there are my grandsons William Miller and Charles Stein, and the newly arrived 'Charlie' Alexandra Berns—a girl—born to Tony and his wife." From this brood may come the new Jack and Charlie to carry on the tradition of the house that the original Jack and Charlie built.

Of all the old-guard restaurants, from Sherry's to the Colony, the Café Chauveron to Le Pavillon, the Stork Club, and Perona's El Morocco, of all these famous places, only "21" remains. It is not merely a place left over from other days, however. It lives, still timely, having moved all the way from the zaniness of the underground twenties through the great depressed terrible thirties, the pent-up emotion of the war years, and the calculated smooth professionalism of the last two decades.

Newcomers to this genial watering hole, Jack's dream of the coffeehouse of the age come true, might sum it up with the words "the best bargain in town," and they're right on that score. But to others of us whose families have known this famed establishment since the dark days of Prohibition, it truly has something that our contemporary society doesn't offer—tradition.

Recipes from "21"

*Written and tested by
Terrance R. Dinan and
Anthony Pedretti,
Chef de Cuisine*

As one can well imagine, "21" is besieged constantly by requests for its "secret" recipes. Here are a few for those who would attempt to re-create the flavor of the Club at home. Although the proportions have been reduced to serve a relatively small number of people, rather than dozens, and the methods adapted to the average kitchen, the recipes are authentic and the ingredients identical to those used at "21." As Jerry Berns tells people who report that these dishes somehow don't taste quite the same prepared at home, "The only ingredient left out is the '21' kitchen!"

DINNER

Ramos Gin Fizz
Pâté Maison
Vichyssoise
Sunset Salad Lorenzo
Striped Bass Poché au Court Bouillon
with Sauce Mousseline
Roast Baby Pheasant
with Sauce Périgourdine
Spinach à la Jack
Rice Pudding
Coffee

DINNER

Dry Martini
Mushrooms à la Daum
Potage St. Germain
Mixed Greens with French Dressing "21"
Cold Salmon "21" with Pressed Cucumbers and Sauce Verte
Escalopes de Veau Charleroi
Zucchini Provençale
Pommes Soufflées
Chocolate Pôt de Crème
Café Diable

LUNCHEON SPECIALTIES

Bloody Mary "21"
Chicken Hash "21"
Omelet "21"
"21" Burger
with Hash-Browned Potatoes
Jack & Charlie's Special Sandwich

179
Recipes for each of the above dishes follow

RAMOS GIN FIZZ

Juice of one lemon
1 heaping teaspoon granulated sugar
1 egg white
1 ounce light cream
2 ounces gin
A few drops of orange-flower water*

Combine all the ingredients in a shaker and shake vigorously. Strain into a chilled 12-ounce Tom Collins glass and add club soda to taste. Serves 1.

*Available at specialty shops.

PATE MAISON "21"

5 lbs. chicken livers, trimmed
½ pound veal, cut into 1-inch cubes
½ pound lean pork, cut into 1-inch cubes
2 cups water (approximately)
2 cups milk (approximately)
½ teaspoon nutmeg
½ teaspoon white pepper
½ teaspoon salt
3 cups rendered chicken fat
⅓ cup minced shallots, sautéed in a tablespoon of butter
2 cloves finely chopped garlic
⅓ cup sherry
5 ounces cognac
4–4½ cups heavy cream

Combine the livers, pork, and veal in a baking dish and add water to cover; allow the meat to soak for 24 hours. Drain and cover the meat with milk; soak for another 24 hours. Pour off the milk and season the meat with the nutmeg, pepper, and salt. Bake the mixture in a 350° oven for 1 hour, draining off the liquid every 20 minutes. After baking, drain again thoroughly. Add the chicken fat, shallots, garlic, and sherry, mixing well by hand. Drain the mixture and pass it through a meat grinder, using the finest blade. Cool the ground mixture by placing the bowl in a larger bowl containing crushed ice. When cool, add the brandy and mix by hand. Gradually add the heavy cream, mixing thoroughly.

Line one or two loaf pans, terrines, or pâté molds (depending on size) with a thin layer of lard and fill with the mixture, covering the top with another layer of lard and a loose cover of aluminum foil. Put each pan into a larger baking pan containing water, which should reach a level about halfway up the sides of the loaf pan. Bake at 350° for 1 hour; remove the foil and bake for another ½ hour until the top is browned. Remove from the oven and, using a board cut to fit inside the loaf pan, press the pâté into a bowl filled with crushed ice. When the pâté has cooled, gently press out any liquid and run a spatula around the sides. Turn the pâté out of the pans, peel off the lard, and scrape away the outside skin. In a large bowl, mix the pâté by hand to distribute the salt from the lard throughout the mixture. Coat the bottom of small crocks or jars with a small amount of melted chicken fat and fill them with the pâté mixture. Seal the top with more chicken fat and refrigerate. The pâté can be stored in the refrigerator for 3–4 weeks.

VICHYSSOISE

½ pound butter
2 medium onions, peeled and sliced
5 small potatoes, peeled and sliced
4 leeks, chopped
2 quarts chicken broth
1 prosciutto bone (or piece of ham bone)
3½ to 4 cups light cream
Salt and pepper to taste
Dash Worcestershire sauce
Dash Tabasco
Pinch nutmeg
Chopped fresh chives

Melt the butter in a large heavy saucepan or kettle. Add the onions, potatoes, and leeks and sauté for 15–20 minutes. Add the chicken broth and the prosciutto (or ham) bone and simmer, covered, for 2 hours until the soup becomes thick. Season with salt and pepper. Remove the bone and strain the soup through a fine sieve. Cool. Slowly add the cream, stirring until the desired consistency is reached. Season with the Worcestershire sauce, Tabasco, and nutmeg. Chill. Serve garnished with chopped chives. Serves 4–5.

SUNSET SALAD WITH LORENZO DRESSING

½ head green cabbage
½ head iceberg lettuce
5 thin slices beef tongue or ham, cooked
1 chicken breast, poached and boned
2 chicken thighs, poached and boned

Cut each of the above ingredients into julienne slices. Combine in a large salad bowl and toss with the Lorenzo dressing.

LORENZO DRESSING

½ cup chili sauce
½ cup chopped watercress
½ cup "21" French dressing

Combine the chili sauce and the watercress. Add French dressing and blend thoroughly. Chill. Serves 4.

STRIPED BASS POCHE AU COURT BOUILLON
WITH SAUCE MOUSSELINE

1 whole bass, 4–5 lbs.

Poaching liquid:
1 quart white wine
1 quart water
¼ cup white vinegar
A bouquet garni of 10 peppercorns, 1 teaspoon dried thyme leaves,
1 bay leaf wrapped in cheesecloth
2 small onions, quartered
1 carrot, coarsely chopped
3 sprigs parsley
2 celery stalks, cut up

1 cup hollandaise sauce (see following recipe)
½ cup whipped heavy cream
Parsley
Lemon slices

Clean and scale the fish, leaving head and skin intact. Lower the fish, preferably resting on a rack, into a poaching pan. Combine the ingredients for the poaching liquid and add to the pan until the fish is covered with liquid; bring to a boil. Lower the heat and simmer, covered, very slowly for about 20 minutes or until the fish is done. (Do not let bubbles break the surface of the liquid; if the heat is too high, the fish may be damaged by the agitation. To test the fish, press with a finger; if it is soft and no longer resistant, the flesh is cooked.) Lift the fish from the liquid and place on a warmed serving platter. Discard the vegetables.

While the fish is cooking, prepare sauce mousseline by folding the whipped cream into the hollandaise. Spoon the sauce over the fish, which has been decorated with parsley sprigs and lemon slices, or serve separately from a sauceboat. Serves 4–6.

HOLLANDAISE SAUCE

1½ lbs. butter (clarified)
5 egg yolks
3 tablespoons cold water
Juice of one lemon
Pinch salt
Pinch cayenne pepper
1 teaspoon Worcestershire sauce
Dash Tabasco

Clarify the butter by heating in the top of a double boiler until melted and then skimming off the sediment. Remove and keep at room temperature. Whip the egg yolks with a wire whisk and add the water. Heat in the top of the double boiler over simmering water, whisking frequently to keep the mixture fluffy. When the mixture has thickened, remove from the heat and gradually add the butter in a slow stream, whipping constantly. When all the butter has been used, add the lemon juice, salt, pepper, Worcestershire, and Tabasco. Continue to whip until the mixture reaches the consistency of custard. Serve the sauce at room temperature as soon as possible. Makes 2 cups.

Note: Egg whites may be refrigerated or frozen for future use or for another dish.

ROAST BABY PHEASANT WITH SAUCE PERIGOURDINE

4 baby pheasants (1½ lbs. each), cleaned and trussed
4 slices of lard
2 tablespoons vegetable oil
2 stalks celery, diced
2 medium carrots, peeled and diced
1 medium onion, peeled and diced
2 bay leaves
Pinch of rosemary
1 cup chicken broth, approximately
4 teaspoons diced truffle
1 ounce sherry
1 ounce cognac
1 teaspoon chopped shallots

Cover the breast of each pheasant with a slice of lard. In a large sauté pan, heat the oil and add the diced vegetables, bay leaves, and rosemary. Lay the pheasants on top of the vegetables and bake in a 350° oven for about 40 minutes, basting occasionally with the chicken broth. When the birds are cooked, remove them to a serving dish and keep warm; reserve the cooking juices. Combine the truffle, sherry, cognac, and shallots in a small saucepan and boil for a few minutes until the liquid is reduced by about half. Strain the cooking juices from the baking pan and pour into the truffle mixture. Simmer over a low flame for about 15 minutes. When ready to serve, pour the sauce over the pheasants. Serve with wild rice and braised celery. Serves 4.

SPINACH A LA JACK

2 lbs. fresh leaf spinach
2 slices bacon
1 tablespoon butter
1 cup heavy cream
Dash nutmeg
Salt and black pepper to taste

Wash and clean the spinach and remove the stalks. Cook in half an inch of boiling salted water until just tender and drain thoroughly. Purée the cooked spinach in a blender. Fry the bacon until crisp; drain on absorbent paper and crumble. Reserve. In a heavy saucepan, melt the butter and add the purée. Stir in the heavy cream and season with nutmeg, salt, and pepper. Simmer over a very low flame for about 15 minutes. Top with the crumbled bacon before serving. Serves 4.

RICE PUDDING

1 quart milk
1 pint heavy cream
½ teaspoon salt
1 vanilla bean
¾ cup raw long-grained rice
1 cup sugar
1 egg yolk
1½ cups whipped cream

In a heavy saucepan, combine the milk, cream, salt, vanilla bean, and ¾ cup of the sugar and bring to a boil. Stirring well, add the rice and allow the mixture to simmer gently, covered, for 1¾ hours over a very low flame, until the rice is soft. Remove from the heat and cool slightly. Blending well, stir in the remaining ¼ cup of sugar and the egg yolk. Allow to cool a bit more. Preheat the broiler. Stirring in all but 2 tablespoons of the whipped cream, pour the mixture into individual earthenware crocks or a soufflé dish. (Raisins may be placed in the bottom of the dishes if desired.) After spreading the remaining whipped cream in a thin layer over the top, place the crocks or dish under the broiler until the pudding is lightly browned. Chill before serving. Serves 10–12.

MUSHROOMS A LA DAUM

2 cups sliced mushrooms
1 cup minced onions
1 cup Danish ham and/or tongue, julienne
Salt and freshly ground black pepper to taste
8 tablespoons (½ cup) sweet butter
¼ cup brown sauce (see recipe on page 187)
Fresh parsley

In a mixing bowl, combine the mushrooms, onions, ham and/or tongue, and seasonings. Melt the butter in a skillet and sauté the mushroom mixture over a medium flame for about 5 minutes, until the mushrooms and onions are soft. Stirring in the brown sauce, heat for 1 more minute. Serve over toast or prepared artichoke bottoms. Garnish with parsley. Serves 4.

POTAGE ST. GERMAIN

2 tablespoons butter
2 small onions, peeled and diced
2 stalks celery, diced
2 medium carrots, peeled and diced
1½ quarts chicken broth
½ lb. dried split peas
A ham bone
Salt and pepper to taste

Melt the butter in a heavy saucepan or kettle and sauté the onions, celery, and carrots for 5–7 minutes. Add the chicken broth, peas, ham bone, and salt and pepper. Bring the liquid to a boil, lower the heat, and cover the pot. Simmer for 1 hour or until the peas are very tender. Strain the soup through a sieve and serve with croutons. Serves 4.

"21" FRENCH DRESSING

1 egg yolk
½ teaspoon Worcestershire sauce (or more, to taste)
1⅓ cups cider vinegar
½ teaspoon paprika (see note)
1 teaspoon dry mustard
1 teaspoon salt
½ teaspoon freshly ground black pepper
2⅔ cups olive oil

Using a whisk, beat into the egg yolks the Worcestershire sauce and about ⅓ cup of the vinegar. Add the paprika, mustard, salt, pepper, and ¼ cup more vinegar and mix well. Gradually, a little at a time, add the olive oil, beating well after each addition until all the oil is incorporated into the vinegar mixture. Add the remaining vinegar, mix well, and serve over freshly washed and dried greens. Makes 1 quart.

Note: The relative amounts of paprika and mustard are optional. If you like a light-colored dressing, use more mustard; if you like it darker, use more paprika.

COLD SALMON "21" WITH
PRESSED CUCUMBERS AND SAUCE VERTE

1 10-lb. salmon

Poaching liquid:
2 quarts dry white wine
1 quart white vinegar
1 gallon water
6 bay leaves
2 pinches thyme leaves
2 lbs. fish bones
3 medium onions, peeled and chopped
6 stalks celery, chopped
Salt and white pepper to taste

Truffles
Olives
Pimentos
Blanched strips of zucchini skin
Tiny shrimp
Sliced lemon
Parsley
2 tablespoons unflavored gelatin

Clean and scale the fish, leaving head and tail intact. Place the fish on a rack and lower into a large poacher. Combine the poaching-liquid ingredients and pour around the fish until it is covered with liquid. Simmer for about 25 minutes, uncovered. Remove the pan from the heat and let the salmon cool in the liquid for about 4 hours. Remove the salmon, peel off and discard the skin, and place the fish on a platter or wooden board. Reserve the poaching liquid. Decorate the fish with the remaining ingredients (except the gelatin), cut up and arranged according to your own design. Chill in the refrigerator for 1 hour.

Add the gelatin to 1 quart of the strained poaching liquid, stirring well until it is dissolved; cool the aspic until it begins to jell. Spoon a layer over the decorated salmon and return the fish to the refrigerator. Chill for ½ hour, then repeat the process three times, chilling between each addition of aspic. (If the aspic becomes too thick to handle, warm it over boiling water until it liquefies.) When ready to serve, cut the aspic around the salmon to separate it from the platter and transfer the fish carefully to a slab of white marble or a serving dish. Decorate with more sliced lemon and parsley. Serve with pressed cucumbers and sauce verte. Serves 6–8.

PRESSED CUCUMBERS

6 cucumbers
2 tablespoons mayonnaise
1 tablespoon lemon juice
Pinch nutmeg
Pepper to taste

Peel and halve the cucumbers lengthwise, removing the seeds. Slice each half-cucumber into ⅛-inch slices. Place the slices in a large sieve, sprinkle with salt, and cover with a weight; set the sieve over a bowl and allow the cucumbers to drain for several hours. When ready to serve, toss the slices with the mayonnaise, lemon juice, nutmeg, and pepper.

SAUCE VERTE

1 cup fresh spinach
½ cup watercress
1 tablespoon chives
½ cup chopped leeks
½ cup parsley
2 cups mayonnaise

Boil the spinach, watercress, chives, leeks, and parsley together for 7 minutes in salted water. Drain well and cool. When the greens are cold, pass them through a grinder. Blend the purée with the mayonnaise and serve with the salmon.

186

ESCALOPES DE VEAU CHARLEROI

8 tablespoons sweet butter
2 medium onions, chopped
1 dozen medium-sized mushrooms, chopped
2 bay leaves
Pinch rosemary
1 cup raw long-grain rice
3 cups water
Salt and freshly ground black pepper to taste
2 egg yolks
2 cups unsweetened whipped heavy cream
½ cup grated Parmesan cheese
8 pieces of pounded veal scallops, about 3½ inches in diameter
½ cup all-purpose flour
½ cup Madeira
1 cup brown sauce (see following recipe)

Preheat the oven to 350°. In a deep casserole, melt 4 tablespoons of the butter and, over a low flame, sauté the onions and mushrooms until softened but not brown (about 10 minutes). Add the bay leaves and rosemary and cook for another 15 minutes, keeping the flame very low. Stirring constantly, add the rice and cook for a moment until it is coated with butter. Slowly stir in the water and season with salt and pepper. When the mixture comes to a boil, cover the casserole and bake in the oven for about 25 minutes, or until the rice is tender. After the mixture has cooled, purée it in a food mill. Beat the egg yolks and add them to the purée, stirring well. Carefully fold in the whipped cream and half of the cheese. Put the mixture into a pastry bag and set aside.

Lightly dip the pounded veal slices in flour, shaking to remove excess. In a large skillet, melt the remaining butter (4 tablespoons) and brown the veal slices on both sides over a medium flame, cooking about 10 minutes in all. Arrange the veal on an oven-proof serving dish and preheat the broiler.

Into the skillet in which the veal was cooked, pour the Madeira and stir well. Boil over a high flame for a few minutes until the juices are reduced by about half. Mixing thoroughly with a whisk, slowly add the brown sauce, and simmer until warmed through. Set aside.

Squeeze the mixture in the pastry bag over the veal, making a crisscross pattern on each piece, and sprinkle the remaining cheese over the top. Place the dish under the broiler until the top is golden brown. The Madeira sauce may be poured onto the serving dish around the veal or served separately. Serves 4–6.

BROWN SAUCE

5 cups strong beef stock
4 tablespoons unsalted butter
4 tablespoons all-purpose flour
1 clove garlic, peeled
1 bay leaf
½ teaspoon dried chopped thyme
1 small onion, chopped
¼ teaspoon Worcestershire sauce
Madeira wine to taste
Salt and freshly ground black pepper to taste

Preheat the oven to 350°. Bring the stock to a boil. In a small heavy-bottomed saucepan, melt the butter and add the flour, blending thoroughly with a whisk. Allow to cook for a few minutes until the mixture is slightly browned. Pour the stock into a casserole dish and stir in the *roux* (butter-flour mixture). Simmer over a low flame until the stock is slightly thickened. Add the garlic, bay leaf, thyme, onion, and Worcestershire sauce and place the casserole in the oven, "roasting" for about 1½ hours. Strain the sauce into a bowl or pan, add the wine, and season to taste with salt and pepper. Makes 1 quart.

ZUCCHINI PROVENCALE

2 tablespoons olive oil
3 tomatoes, peeled and chopped
1 finely chopped clove of garlic
4 medium-sized zucchini
2 tablespoons butter
Salt and black pepper to taste

Heat the olive oil in a heavy saucepan and add the tomatoes and garlic, sautéing over a low flame for about 15 minutes. Meanwhile, slice the zucchini and sauté in butter in a separate pan until tender and lightly browned. Add the tomato-garlic mixture to the zucchini and simmer for 5 minutes. Season to taste. Serves 4.

POMMES SOUFFLEES

4 large Idaho potatoes
Vegetable oil for deep frying
Salt

After peeling the potatoes, slice them crosswise about ⅛ inch thick. Trim the slices into uniform oval shapes 4 to 5 inches long and 1½ inches wide. Soak the slices in cold water for about 20 minutes. Drain and dry well. Fill a heavy pot half full with oil and gradually heat to a temperature of 250°. Carefully drop the potato slices into the oil. When they rise to the surface, slowly agitate the pot, setting up a wavelike motion of the oil; continue this step for about 10 minutes. When the potatoes become somewhat opaque toward the center, remove them from the pot with a wire basket or slotted spoon and drain on absorbent paper, allowing them to cool for at least 5 minutes (see note). Just before serving, reheat the oil to a temperature of 375°. Drop the slices into the oil one by one and again agitate the pot with a wire basket or slotted spoon and drain on absorbent paper, allowing absorbent paper. Sprinkle with salt and serve. (If the potatoes do not seem crisp or puffed enough, return them to the hot oil for a few seconds.) Serves 4.

Note: The first step in frying may be done well ahead of serving and the potatoes refrigerated in the meantime.

CHOCOLATE POT DE CREME

1 pint light cream
½ cup granulated sugar
4 egg yolks
1 whole egg
1 drop vanilla extract
Pinch of salt
2½ ounces bitter chocolate
Whipped cream

Heat the cream until it is hot but not boiling. Stir in half of the sugar. In a separate saucepan, beat the egg yolks and the whole egg. Add the remaining sugar, the vanilla, and the salt. Slowly pour the heated cream into the eggs, stirring constantly. Melt the chocolate in a heavy saucepan over a low flame and very slowly add half the cream-egg mixture, stirring constantly. Add the rest of the mixture, stir, and strain through a fine sieve. Pour into individual ceramic or glass serving dishes and place them in a shallow pan of hot water. Bake in a 225° oven for 20 minutes. Chill. Top with whipped cream. Serves 4–6.

CAFE DIABLE

Peel of one lemon (removed in a single strip)
Peel of one orange (removed in a single strip)
24 cloves
2 sticks cinnamon
2 teaspoons granulated sugar
3 8-ounce cups espresso coffee
2 ounces Kirschwasser

Stud the lemon and orange peels with the cloves and add them to a lined copper bowl with the cinnamon, sugar, and brandy. Set a match to the mixture so that the brandy burns for a moment or two and then add the coffee, putting out the flames. Remove the peels and the cinnamon; add the Kirschwasser. Serve immediately in café diable or demitasse cups. Serves 4 with 6-ounce cups and 8 with demitasse cups.

BLOODY MARY "21"

1½ ounces vodka, chilled
2 ounces tomato juice, chilled
Dash Worcestershire sauce
Salt and black pepper
Celery salt
Tabasco (optional)

Combine the vodka and tomato juice in a shaker and season to taste with Worcestershire, salt, pepper, and celery salt. Shake well and pour into a chilled cocktail glass. Serves 1.

CHICKEN HASH

1 cup béchamel sauce (see following recipe)
½ cup light cream
¼ cup sherry
2 cups cooked white meat of chicken, diced
2 egg yolks

In a saucepan, combine the béchamel and the cream, whipping with a whisk until fluffy. Add the sherry and mix well. Stirring in the chicken, cook over a low heat until the mixture is hot. Correct seasoning. Stir in the egg yolks, blending well with a spoon. Serve hot over toast, waffle, a baked potato shell, or wild rice, or incorporated into an omelet or a crêpe. Serves 4.

BECHAMEL SAUCE

2 cups milk
2 tablespoons butter
2 tablespoons flour
¼ teaspoon white pepper
Salt to taste
Dash Tabasco
Dash Worcestershire sauce

Preheat the oven to 300°. Scald the milk. Melt the butter in a heavy-bottomed saucepan with a metal handle. Add the flour, stirring with a whisk for a couple of minutes. Gradually stir in the milk and continue to whisk until the mixture is thickened. Season with the pepper, salt, Tabasco, and Worcestershire sauce and place the saucepan, covered, in the preheated oven. After allowing it to bake for about 1½ hours, strain the sauce, which should be very thick and fluffy in consistency. Correct the seasoning. Makes 1½ cups.

Mornay Sauce: Follow the instructions above, adding ¼–½ cup of grated Parmesan or Swiss cheese to the mixture when you season it before placing in the oven.

OMELET "21"

1 tablespoon butter
3 eggs
Dash salt
½ cup Chicken Hash "21" (see preceding recipe)
½ cup Mornay sauce (see preceding recipe)
¼ cup grated Parmesan cheese

Preheat the broiler. While melting the butter in an omelet pan, beat the eggs with a whisk and season with salt. When the butter is foamy, add the eggs and allow them to settle for a moment. As the sides become firm, draw them into the center with a fork, repeating this step until the omelet is nearly done but still moist in the center. Add the chicken hash. After another few moments, roll the omelet out onto a warmed serving dish, and spoon the sauce down the center of the rolled omelet. Dust with Parmesan cheese and set the omelet under the broiler until the cheese turns golden brown. Serve immediately. Serves 1.

"21" BURGER

2 pounds ground sirloin
¼ teaspoon nutmeg
Dash Worcestershire sauce
Salt and freshly ground black pepper to taste
¼ cup bread crumbs
¼ cup cooked celery, chopped fine

Preheat the oven to 350°. In a mixing bowl, combine all of the ingredients by hand, using rapid motions, without overworking mixture. Shape into round patties (about 8–10 ounces each). Heat a little vegetable oil in a skillet with a metal handle. When the pan is very hot, brown the patties quickly on both sides. Put the skillet in the oven and cook the meat until done to taste (about 5 minutes for rare). Serves 3–4.

HASH-BROWNED POTATOES

1 pound potatoes
2 tablespoons butter

Peel and clean the potatoes; boil in salted water until tender but not mushy. Drain. Let the potatoes cool, then cut into small dice. Heat the butter in a frying pan; when hot, add the potatoes. Flatten the potatoes with a spatula and season with salt and pepper. When the bottom of the potato layer has browned, turn and cook until the other side becomes golden brown. Serve immediately. Serves 4.

JACK & CHARLIE'S SPECIAL SANDWICH

2 slices smoked turkey
2 slices Virginia ham
1 slice Pâté Maison (see recipe, page 180)
2 slices rye toast

Layer the slices of meat on one slice of the toast and top with the second piece of toast. Serve with sweet gherkins and beer. Serves 1.